Carved in Stone

by

Melanie Jackson

Version 1.3 – February, 2015

Discover other titles by Melanie Jackson at
www.melaniejackson.com

ISBN 978-1508492191

Printed in the United States of America

Table of Contents

Chapter One

San Francisco was an assault after the quiet of Bartholomew's Woods, and not even the muffling fog could cushion the sounds of traffic and voices, and the smells of exhaust and thousands of highly spiced dinners that were trapped between the tall buildings that lined the narrow alleys leading up to the hill where the castle squatted. The city below it had marched right up to the water and to the highest peak of the nearby mountains without hesitation or thought of the consequences.

Juliet would not have minded going for a walk, but the neighborhood around Paul House was appallingly expensive, did not want tourists, and therefore was not pedestrian friendly. Juliet thought it should have been called Valhalla or Olympus or something grand. Locally it was known as the Heights.

"The heights of bad taste," she muttered and then looked around to see she wasn't overheard.

There were compensations to being so far up the hill and away from the city bustle. The wind wasn't blowing, which was nice because it could be a real bully when it came from the north. The last of the daylight that surrounded the ramparts was also spectacular, an eerie luminosity that happened when the sun and fog did battle at the end of the day. The contest between the human mundane and Nature's divinity couldn't be more pronounced, and very few people on the planet would ever have the privilege of witnessing the phenomenon from her location. It was easy to imagine that she was looking over some vast kingdom, though it was more a kingdom of verticals than sprawls. The one-way streets, many steep and narrow, tended to make the city feel larger than it was. She couldn't help but admire the sheer stubbornness of the people who lived there in spite of common sense and daily inconvenience.

That did not mean that she wanted to stay.

Juliet had received the invitation to San Francisco with all the enthusiasm she would feel for attending a public execution, but Raphael had seemed to truly want her company—or perhaps wanted to stop her hiding out, which she had been doing since the modern art show and the death of her old NSA instructor, Jessop Carmody. Whatever Raphael's motivation was, she had accepted the invitation and then packed her duffel with dark, wrinkle-resistant clothing without making any outward complaint. He already knew how she felt about billionaires and their toys. Juliet had always lived in modest quarters even when she had had a steady salary. Her comfort zone of domestic space made her prefer buildings smaller than castles. No matter how renovated the space or cordial the owner, she would never feel at home in the places where Raphael frequently stayed.

That did not mean that she couldn't manage a short visit if it pleased him, she assured herself.

Thankfully it was quiet and odorless inside Paul House, which had turned out to be rather more interesting than expected. The so-called house, truth to be told, was a little like a museum, its atmosphere pleasantly stale and slightly chilled. Actually, on an overcast day, it was more like a mausoleum or a crypt in a cathedral that tourists never visited. Aesthetically, Juliet could and did admire the ancient stones of various edifices that had been brought over block by block and then Frankensteined into a new and more useful structure. It was impressive as castles were wont to be, but not on such a scale that mere humans couldn't walk through it without uncomfortable levels of intimidation. Still, the architecture had been originally produced under some baroque circumstances that did not fit modern needs or tastes. At least not her modern tastes. Perhaps the very wealthy were different.

Still, could the new owner really plan to live there? It seemed too gloomy a spot for such a charming man who claimed to love his small Paris apartment. Juliet found herself longing more each day for her own home, which was more suited to a maiden lady and a cat who were both happy to dine on tuna at her small and rather worn breakfast-sized table. Wouldn't he feel the same after a while? The place was large and … kind of creepy.

Ancient Paul House was not her thing, though she didn't think that she was psychic or even particularly sensitive to auras and vibrations. Still one couldn't help but be aware that the stones had absorbed centuries of deaths, dark deeds, and hard times, and sometimes the knowledge crept into her dreams just before she woke and made her uneasy. No, she wouldn't want to live there, not even with the pretty creepers that clung to its medieval façade, softening its hard lines.

Juliet shook her head, trying to shake off the feeling of melancholy that sometimes arrived with the sunset. Especially when she was alone. She was turning peculiar and Raphael deserved better of her than a mopey face when he was enjoying himself so much.

Paul House was more aesthetically pleasing than the castle-temple she had seen in Mexico. Raphael had pointed this out their first day at Paul House when he sensed her dislike. It was the result of a burst of creative affluence of another era when excesses in bad taste were celebrated instead of deplored, and it was not inherently disturbing to the artistic senses—and the owner was not a Nazi war criminal, which had to be looked upon as a huge improvement over their last castle, which had been tainted by a kind of psychic miasma and a definite Nazi presence.

The San Francisco castle did resemble the fortress in Mexico in one respect. It was a hybrid. In places the floor plan hesitated, and even when the stonework had been made to match, it was evident that one was standing at a grafting point where one building flowed into another.

Maybe this was what was bothering her. She was visiting the sins of her Mexico trip upon another grandiose structure.

Besides, whatever her remaining misgivings about their surroundings, Raphael was completely immersed in restoring the frescoes in the ground floor chapel, and Juliet was amassing an impressive collection of gargoyle paintings and sketches which she could put to good use come Halloween. Most were spooky and would appeal to those with gothic tastes, but some of the wall dragons were actually fairly amusing looking and these she would screen onto t-shirts and trick-or-treat bags.

And Bertram Fröndenberger and his flourishing chin hair and myopic eyes would be arriving soon. He and Raphael were part of the small brotherhood of those who practiced the esoteric arts. They were men of exquisite patience, discernment, and talent. They did nothing and thought nothing and certainly said nothing in a slapdash manner. Juliet, who was also precise in her thoughts, appreciated this trait.

Juliet hadn't seen Bertram since her stay in Mexico the previous year. He was going to work on restoring the altar pieces which had been slightly damaged in the '06 quake. Actually, it had been damaged before that and mended at the time of the sixteenth-century peasants' uprising in Germany. The artist, Tilman Marienberg, had been a follower of the philosopher Thomas Müntzer and had joined with the peasants when they rose up against the church because of its nasty habit of taxing the lower classes into starvation. He had sympathized with their questioning whether the edicts of the church were truly God's will and if it was necessary to have priests interceding with God. He had probably not counted on the peasants looting and burning the church where his masterpiece was housed. At least he had not been tortured like his fellow artist that shared his first name, Tilman Riemenschneider.

While not as good an artist as Riemenschneider, Marienberg also worked in the

Mannerist style and this made his pieces very lifelike and appealing. Every person on that altar piece had been a real, living, breathing person and not some generic saint or angel pulled out of the artist's head. Juliet found it fascinating. It was worth the finest and most detailed efforts of restoration. De Smet must have felt that too, because for what he was spending on restoration he could have had new pieces cast in solid gold and adorned with precious stones and then polished with the hair of virgins.

De Smet. The owner of the house was also fascinating and every bit the *rara avis* as any of the works of art within the castle. Alain De Smet was a Belgian expatriate with lots of money, lots of whimsy, and the time to indulge his hobbies now that he was semi-retired. His latest enthusiasm was taking over the long abandoned Paul House and restoring its all but forgotten treasures now that the very expensive retrofit was mostly done and the building was safe from earthquakes. Well, safer. As Juliet had learned since moving to California, when the dragon rolled over, no one was truly safe.

Renovations had come a long way. She understood that when he had first seen the castle it had been in a state that would frighten a lunatic. Unless it was the lunatic groundskeeper who had been living alone in the once sumptuous Bedlam by then turning into squalor with his increasing insanity ground into the accumulating grime.

The ridiculously handsome De Smet, who had the classic kind of rugged looks that made people want to vote for him or sign him up to star in major movies, was not married, having failed to find the right woman to slip into the marital harness where she would have to run nonstop to complete the domestic team he envisioned. Or so he said the one night he had come upon her while she was working and stayed for a visit. He had confessed his supposed loneliness with twinkling eyes which belied his tale of a lonely heart. Juliet tried to imagine what such a superwoman might be like and failed. Such a paragon of beauty, brains, manners, and tolerance for the endless quirky causes simply didn't exist anymore. De Smet would need to find a time machine and go back to the fifties when they were still making the Grace Kelly model.

But then, he was a multimillionaire, maybe billionaire. Probably he would find the right woman when he was ready, or arrange to have one manufactured. Or cloned. He was invested in a lot of tech companies. Probably one of them could arrange the perfect specimen from ancient DNA.

Allowing for the fact that De Smet's charm was rather like the San Francisco fog, soft but all encompassing, and that people tended to want to move wherever his spirit listed, a trait she did not trust or like, Juliet still found that she was drawn to him. She had also learned that same night that De Smet still owned his soul. He had explained, without a twinkle, that the markets had grown disgustingly predatory, run by computers programmed with algorithms that were as soulless as the people who profited from the often rigged trading. Then the billionaire investors bought up companies only to rend them to pieces and leave the less attractive divisions floating like chum in the water, which attracted other sharks that gobbled up employee pension plans and put whole towns out of work. There was no room for human intuition or intervention when the machine began rolling. The world he had inhabited for twenty years was no longer entertaining. It had become a blood sport for sociopaths. Having enough—more than enough—money, he had decided to retire from active trading and find some other way to enjoy life.

Juliet respected this. It took courage to walk away from what one knew and to take on a new life with all new challenges. Not everyone could do it, and she recognized and appreciated a fellow traveler on the road to personal and professional discovery. She didn't know if she would have the chance to talk to him again, but hoped that Fate would arrange it. He was the best thing about Paul House.

"But he's not here now."

And perhaps that was a good thing. There was danger in being around those special beings who could assure whole groups of people that were collectively the most charming, beautiful, and witty creatures that had ever walked the earth. And, in turn, these flattered groups were willing to do anything to please the person that had made them feel smart and sexy etc. So much charm should not be loosed on one bored woman in close quarters. She liked to think she was above being influenced but didn't feel like putting the matter to the test.

Juliet was standing next to a pile of tarped lumber and scaffolding that had come up from the

11

lowest reaches of the house earlier that day. It rather resembled a giant huddling beneath covers, perhaps having fainted upon reaching fresh air. The vaguely human-shaped pile rather ruined the charming effect of the sunset and the crenellations of the wall that surrounded the estate, so she kept her eyes on the colorful horizon and away from the modern equipment that supposedly kept them safe from the titans under the earth.

The last space in Paul House that the workmen vacated was the *basement* which they had been using for storage of tools and building supplies, and much of it was piled in the very wide driveway. It turned out, of course, that the castle didn't have just a garden-variety basement lurking in the nether regions. Certainly the average basement might be full of tools and paint cans, or perhaps canning jars or kid's cast-off toys. But the lower levels of Paul House were also filled with crypts. Crypts without bodies, or so she was assured when she asked De Smet, but still grave markers that told at least partial stories of the inhabitants of one of the castles that had been purloined by the improbably named R. Paul Diamond III and brought to the United States to be his ostentatious home. Juliet doubted that Mr. Diamond was entitled to the III at the end of his name, but there was no denying that he had been a big shot in San Francisco at the time of the raucous birth of the Barbary Coast. Juliet had been intrigued enough by the house to do some research on the first owner.

Juliet wondered if this opening of the nether regions would bring back the rather unpleasant old man from the historical society, Addison Smith, who was opposed to every effort of the renovation. Juliet had only met him once but had heard some of the staff talking about him and his creepy habit of showing up in the kitchens and pantry where he really had no business to be. Juliet tried to think nice thoughts about him, like maybe he was just hungry or looking for a cup of coffee without disturbing anyone, but she rather wished that he would stay away from the kitchens since his appearance nearly always set off the cook who had taken a real aversion to him. When the cook was unhappy, everyone else was affected too.

Another of the less fascinating occupants of Paul House was Marcus Trent, the artisan who was cleaning and restoring the stained glass and tapestry at the front of the house. Marcus was a loner and difficult to read for several reasons. He had had a facelift—a rather extreme one—but somehow one could see the old face underneath, trying to get out and bleeding through the taut skin like ink leaking out from under a cheap coat of paint. The skin of his nose was slightly keratotic, speaking of careless days in the sun, and he wore his hair affectedly unkempt. It was a youthful style that was dated to the pop bands of the early eighties and would have been, even then, still too young for the hard eyes that looked out of that unnaturally smooth face. He also tended to speak in a monotone, when he spoke at all. He was under a deadline because the tapestries were coming back later that week, and they could not be hung until he was done with the nearby windows that required extensive leading.

The historic textiles had been taken away for cleaning and careful repair but were due to make their twenty-first century debut appearance at the coming Valentine's Ball, which was a fundraiser for Alain De Smet's favorite charity that supported music programs in disadvantaged schools.

And that left the cleaning staff, gardeners, and the new cook, who was very good at her job when De Smet was in residence, but such an unpleasant person the rest of the time that everyone in the castle had taken to avoiding her. She went by the name of Marigold, a self-selected name she had made legal some years ago, and one which confused Juliet. If there was ever a person who was not sunny and cute, it was the chef De Smet had brought with him to San Francisco.

Juliet would have been content to slip into the kitchen between meals and prepare tuna sandwiches for their lunch. Tuna was simple but real. Unlike microwave meals which tasted like the supposed food had been subjected to dangerous industrial processing before being plopped on the plastic-covered tray that always seemed to crisp around the edges no matter how low the radiation setting. But Marigold had made it plain that intruders at any time of day and for any reason were not welcome in her domain.

Juliet had seen the skinny viper hove into view while sketching the back stair and she watched the staff once again dissolve into the woodwork, leaving their tasks unfinished rather than face her. Thinking it best to absent herself as well, Juliet decided that it would be nice to watch the sunset from outside where Marigold rarely ventured. And it was a good choice even if it was rather chilly. At least she would not have to smell the pungent and nearly medicinal lavender scent that the cook always wore.

The image that always came to mind when Marigold was on the warpath was Scottish monks scattering at the sight of a Viking ship on the horizon. Or maybe she was thinking about the psalm, the one that talked about the venom of snakes being under their tongues. Whatever the analogy, anyone not able to escape in time was doomed. Marigold would reach into her quiver of insults and complaints and begin her barrage, usually in two languages. Hearing the personal tirades made Juliet recall with increasing unease what could happen when someone set about deliberately and systematically making enemies. It wasn't good.

But this domestic bickering was not her business. Marigold had said nothing to her directly, and Juliet would not play busybody and interfere with the household arrangements. Other than to avoid witnessing any more embarrassing scenes with the staff, of course. Those put her teeth on edge.

The sunset's peace was destroyed by the sound of someone squashing a soda can, stomping on it like it was a cockroach then tossing it into the recycling bin kept at the side of the castle where the stables had been turned into a garage. The day workers were packing up and getting ready to head home.

Realizing that she was getting cold and that enough time had elapsed for Marigold to have annihilated half of the domestic employees, Juliet abandoned her inspection of the city as it surrendered to a rare winter fog. She also gave up all thoughts of having pancakes for dinner. She had been craving them, but the best pancakes in town were on the wrong side of the great divide, and the river of traffic that was Van Ness Avenue stood between her and her heart's desire. This busy road bisected the city and psychics believed it was a kind of ley line. It was historic fact that the houses along Van Ness had been dynamited after the earthquake of '06 in an effort to save the rest of the city from fire that was raging out of control. There had been protests about this—naturally—and the echoes of old violence and horror lingered along the thoroughfare. Or so the books she had read the night before insisted. What was a certainty was that Van Ness divided the city physically and Juliet had learned that one did not undertake a crossing without careful planning, especially when there was fog. She had tried it and discovered that it was as though left turns were the ultimate traffic sin and totally forbidden, and there seemed to be a never ending supply of one-way streets traveling in the wrong direction of where she wanted to go. The road was difficult to cross at all hours, but impossible once rush hour started.

However, food was a must. According to her personal tracker, she had walked over eleven thousand steps and climbed a dozen flights of stairs. Juliet had eaten only lightly at lunch and was ravenous enough to raid the larder, Marigold or no Marigold. But only as a last resort. Surely Raphael would also be ready for dinner and they could get something warm and carb-heavy.

They did not dress for the evening most nights, since they were all tired by nightfall and they did not dine formally when De Smet was away; but Juliet needed to add a sweater to her already layered clothing before venturing out, and that could be something elegant. That meant a trip to the third floor. There was an elevator of sorts, but she always took the stairs unless in Raphael's company. That meant that she would log at least fifteen flights of stairs for the day. Paul House was certainly keeping her in shape.

Her room in the east wing was very nice if a bit austere. An effort had been made to soften the expanse of hard stone by supplying some rugs and the few heavy tables with vases of flowers. The blooms were beginning to be past their prime though, and the scent of sweet decay ascended from the drooping roses as they translated from life into death. She would have to do something with the flowers by the next day if the staff did not see to it.

Juliet pulled on one of Rose's lacy alpaca wraps. They were very soft and warm. It would also smell a bit of animal when it got damp, but not unpleasantly so.

There was a familiar tap on the door almost at once, and Juliet smiled as she let Raphael into her borrowed bedroom. The doors were all large, grand enough to ride a horse through without scraping either your plumed helmet or armored knees.

Raphael was always meticulous about his appearance and she wondered how long it had taken him to get the blue pigment off of his hands. Raphael mixed his own paints to match ancient recipes and sometimes it got a little messy. Not that she minded a bit of paint. She had catalogued his whole library of scars. None of them mattered to her except the one that had bisected his spine. But since it did not seem to trouble him she never spoke of the distress it would cause her if she let it flower.

"I know our dining options are limited…." he began. Juliet nodded. The food that Marigold produced might be more than edible, but the formal dining room had all the warmth—and cheerless lighting—of a funeral parlor and they had taken to avoiding meals there when they could.

The more modern eateries in the area tended to have signs without punctuation and phonetic spelling of bad puns. The food was also marginal at best unless you went hardcore ethnic.

"But Marigold is in crisis again and I would rather have Thai food anyway," Juliet said. The Thai restaurant was close and on flat ground. San Francisco had old neighborhoods and buildings that were not wheelchair friendly. The food was also spicy enough to make her breath flammable, but Raphael didn't seem to mind.

"How would you feel about a fatted calf and Bertram's company instead?"

"He's arrived?" she asked with pleased surprise. "I must have missed him coming in."

"Yes, he's here and I thought we would spare him and the staff the uneasy dinner preparations.

And also the *panang* since his digestion isn't what it used to be."

"Sounds fine. Shall we take my car? You were thinking of Adam's Steak House maybe?"

The décor at Adam's was more viva Italia than typical ranch style. In fact, the décor cried out for an opera-singing tenor and candles melting in Chianti bottles, but what they had was Dean Martin and Frank Sinatra, mercifully played at acceptably quiet levels. And there was no worry about finding rat droppings nestled among the capers or cockroaches in the soup. The same could not be said of some of the other local eateries on the same street. And, the most important feature, they would not have to cross Van Ness to reach it.

"Yes and yes, that might be best. Bertram rented a car, but I am pretty sure that he should not be driving it."

Juliet shook her head as she reached for her purse. Bertram was half-blind. She didn't know how he still had a license. If in fact he had one at all.

They stopped by Bertram's room and collected him before taking the recently installed service elevator down to the ground floor and then cutting through the baking kitchen to the garage. It had once been a stable, but part of the conversion had been to make the stalls into spaces wide enough for automobiles.

Bertram was in a jovial mood and unbent enough to ask Juliet if she had seen any ghosts at Paul House. Their last meeting had required Juliet to play the role of someone who believed in curses and hauntings, so she was not too surprised by the question.

"I haven't met up with any specters yet. But if there are ghosts, I imagine they are happy to be in San Francisco in the twenty-first century and not stuck in their own eras of plagues and burning heretics at the stake."

"Yes, yes—assuming they are aware, of course. I should think they would be much happier here. There is even fog."

There was indeed fog and Juliet was glad that they would not need to travel far in it. It seemed like the kind of night best spent curled up by the fire with friends and a bottle of wine. Perhaps she should suggest that.

"The castle does have one fright though," Juliet said, waiting for the chance to make a left turn.

"That woman with the red hair who snarls at everyone? Yes, I have met her."

"Her name is Marigold and she is an excellent chef—but a rather inadequate human. But, on the bright side, she might very well keep all the ghosts away."

"She will keep people away too." Bertram changed the subject. "I wish to have scorched ribs. That is a local delicacy?"

"Barbecued ribs, and yes, the steak house does good ones. They are served with coleslaw."

"*Was is das?*"

"A sort of cabbage salad," Juliet explained.

"And French fried potatoes," Raphael added.

"I have had those—*pommes frites*—but I do not think they are French at all."

"Most likely not, but you will probably like them anyway. They have garlic and truffle oil."

"Truffles. That is something good from France. That and their opera."

Chapter Two

Juliet looked out her window as she brushed her hair. The morning sky was swollen with clouds that moved sluggishly. The sea damp had left dew on everything, making things appear especially dark with dread in the dim morning light. It was not a day for perching on ledges and enjoying the great outdoors while she sketched. Juliet decided it was time to explore the crypts and their funerary sculpture, which had been serving as a storehouse of building supplies and had been off limits until then. If she was lucky, there would be something new to draw.

Her intention to explore the netherworld was announced over tea and toast in the grotesquely oversized dining room where they gathered to break their fast, and Juliet was surprised when Raphael and Bertram asked to join her.

She suspected that it was partly gallantry on Bertram's part, who no doubt thought she would be nervous near the now empty graves and who was also waiting for his tools to arrive—they had been rerouted to Hawaii when he went through customs in Maine and would not be back on the west coast until nearly ten o'clock. But it was pure curiosity for Raphael, who knew her rather better than Bertram and would have felt fine leaving her to her own devices if he had been uninterested in seeing the imported houses of the dead.

"Of course. The more the merrier. It should be interesting to see the medieval carvings." Or so she hoped.

Bertram grunted, showing that he did not think there would be anything merry about the crypts. He was probably right, but Juliet was undaunted. Funerary art was often some of the most moving and fascinating of sculptures, and she had learned a fair amount about it at the Memento Mori Museum while assisting Esteban at one of his shows.

Thankfully, the stair to the crypt was reasonably wide and two of the charmed staff were able to carry Raphael's chair down, walking side by side while they conversed shyly with their hero.

Juliet found herself uneasy as they descended the stairs. She knew that the house had been made as safe as possible, but the strange frescos and mosaics added to the vaulted ceiling did not have any visible means of support except the cracked cement they had been embedded in.

"Those are not medieval," Bertram said with heavy disapproval.

"No. They look Victorian. And bad Victorian at that."

They looked a Victorian mess. Someone had embedded gilded cherubs into the plaster which had been decorated with blue paint and mirrors, perhaps trying to suggest a heavenly host floating around the starry sky. But they had been careless, and some of the angels were missing fingers and noses and many had lost their golden luster.

"Hmph!" Bertram did not care for "modern" art, which anything after the seventeenth century was, at least according to his definition.

23

"The crypts are much older," she soothed as the workmen said their goodbyes and went back to whatever they were doing.

The ceiling was high in the crypt, making the space feel cavernous in comparison to the stairs with their low-hanging cherubs. It was definitely cold, but that was to be expected when everything was made of brass, bronze, and stone. Juliet didn't know how they had managed to electrify the space but the Moorish lamps on the wall, while dim, did provide a steady if inadequate light.

There were more angels down there, but these were older. Though truly antique, Juliet didn't much care for them, especially not the large one which she assumed was Gabriel blowing the last trumpet that would call the dead back to heavenly life. He didn't look especially happy to be summoning up the souls of whoever had been sleeping down in the crypt when he was stationed at the door, and it was telling that in his other hand he held a sword.

After glancing at Gabriel, Bertram went at once to study the effigies on the tombs, murmuring to himself in German. Juliet remained with Raphael, taking in the space and trying to imagine what it had been intended to convey. Not comfort. There were angels near the arches that marked the various niches where there were tombs, but they were rather ugly and carried more swords which they seemed to be pointing at the stairs that led into the sepulcher. Maybe they had suspected that this lot of dead souls was not anxious to go and face judgment. Or maybe they just didn't like people visiting their domain and were ordering the living away.

"Humans, go home," Juliet muttered.

"Yes, I feel rather unwanted," Raphael said softly. "What on earth could anyone have wanted with this space?"

"Maybe it was a buy one get one."

Juliet looked at the graves and the plaques embedded in the floor. None of them were dripping with sentiment. These were people who were honored to the degree required by their lineage, but they had not been missed by whoever chose their epitaphs.

"Yeah. It's like … these seem like tombs designed for wealthy but not very nice people. Look at that one with the snake wrapped around the man's feet. Yuck. I prefer the Victorian sentimentality. Maybe that's why Diamond put in that rather awful fresco on the stairs. Anything to lighten up the place."

"Not to make sweeping generalizations—" Raphael said. "But isn't that what we are looking at? People who no one, not even their descendants, cared about enough to keep their graves intact? They allowed an American to come and rob the dead."

"Yeah. A lot of the wealthy barons of the age weren't especially nice. But … this feels weird. Whoever bothered to tell the truth about their families? The richer, the more sanctified they had to appear to be—especially if the family was paying the bills. This is odd. Could the families have died out completely?"

"Yes, that is one explanation." He didn't sound like he accepted it.

25

"Of course, the rich still aren't very nice, come to think of it. I'll grant De Smet an exception, of course." Juliet focused on one grave that did not have an effigy. She walked forward and bent down to examine the name carved on the lid. It had been damaged by blows and by fire. "Well … that's really weird."

"Poor woman," Raphael said as he leaned forward and read the plaque that marked her ridiculously small and plain sarcophagus which had no angels guarding it.

"It is so small," Bertram said, joining them. "I cannot quite see. Was she a child?"

As he peered at the inscription Juliet obligingly shone her flashlight on the old stone, though it might not help all that much since it had been defaced sufficiently that she and Raphael had trouble reading it.

"No. She was a woman. But there never was a body in this grave."

"What do you mean?" Bertram asked.

" 'It is setting a high value upon our opinions to roast men alive on account of them,' " Raphael said quietly after Juliet read the inscription aloud. "She was executed and not allowed in a sanctified grave. This is just a memorial. I wonder if they all are."

Juliet nodded, recognizing the quote by Montaigne. He had been a voice of reason in a very violent and paranoid age.

She touched the edge of the small crypt and was surprised when the lid wobbled slightly. The stone was not seated properly.

"Good God," Bertram said, recoiling when he felt the stone move under his hand. He looked frightened enough that Juliet wondered if he actually thought some ghost was going to emerge from the grave. That was a ridiculous idea, but the crypt was the kind of place where such thoughts could occur.

"But what a morbid thing to have here. Why would anyone buy such a thing? Why would anyone sell it? That is … blasphemous."

"Perhaps it is not so odd. Maybe the first owner didn't read Latin and didn't know what he had bought," Raphael said. "Diamond was wealthy but I haven't heard anyone say he was especially educated. Or possessed with good taste. And the family was probably just as happy to have this blot on the family escutcheon gone."

"Or maybe he just pitied her," Juliet said softly. "I surely do. I know it would be stupid to bring flowers, but I kind of feel like making some kindly gesture."

Raphael nodded.

"We should go," Bertram insisted, still looking upset. "There is nothing of artistic value down here. I do not know why anyone would want to purchase such atrocities. The man must have possessed a sick mind."

"Wait a moment. I want to take a better look at this stone. It's loose and not lined up quite right, I'm afraid it may fall if we get an earthquake," Juliet said, squatting down to examined how the lid was misaligned. Something had been caught between the sides and the top, wedging it open on one side.

"Perhaps the workmen dislodged it. Or an earthshaker," Bertram suggested. He added reluctantly, "We should move it back into place so it will not be damaged if there is another temblor. But then we must leave."

"Wait!" Juliet said as he reached for the sarcophagus cover. She shone her light into the small crack on the right side. A small bit of what looked like leather and something metallic was caught on the lip of the sarcophagus, preventing the lid from settling into its proper groove. There were also a few threads—strands of something red and glossy. Juliet exhaled slowly. "I think … I think there is something … someone in there. I see hair."

Red hair. Gooseflesh rose on her arms. They had not seen the cook at breakfast.

"What? But Mr. De Smet assured us that these graves were empty. That nothing had been desecrated." Bertram sounded shocked.

"I don't think this is the original occupant … help me shift this just a bit so I can see a little more." Her voice was steady though she was not.

Bertram was reluctant but did as she asked. They moved the cover as far as they could without risking it falling, with Raphael steadying the far side as best he could. Had the grave not been so tiny they would never have managed the task without tools.

Bertram blinked and said something sacrilegious in German as he peered at the corpse.

28

Bodies are found by people in all kinds of unexpected places. In abandoned buildings. In forests. On jogging trails in parks. In cars.

It shouldn't be that shocking to find one in a crypt.

Except the crypt was supposed to be empty. The only one who had any claim to that space had died centuries ago and had stayed in Spain, literally turned ashes to ashes and dust to dust by the people who killed her. So they didn't just have a dead body, they had an intruder corpse.

"I don't suppose we can just drop the stone back in place and pretend we didn't find anything." But even as she spoke, Juliet heard her old instructor at the NSA saying *Observe! What do you see?* And she ceased being solely an artist looking for material to paint and became a trained observer taking in the details from the startling to the mundane. Some of her observances wanted to ricochet off emotion, but she refused to be provoked or distracted until the inventory was done. She let the arcane information-gathering apparatus compile its observations, ranking them as a first responder would when performing triage.

The body was not fresh. But it was also not old enough to be the woman whose name was carved on the lid.

There was no odor to speak of and for this Juliet was thankful. The woman was dry, almost mummified. She was also naked, folded tightly into the small space. There was nothing else in the tiny box except for a thin leather belt around her thin neck which bore ligature marks. Had her face expressed horror and desperation, it would have been natural if unpleasant to see. The fact that her mouth was shut, probably hiding a distended tongue, and that her eyes were closed, suggested that someone had taken the time to do that much for her before packing her into the grave and dropping a stone over her.

Juliet would ascribe possible motives to this act later. For the moment, she wanted to concentrate on the physical aspects of the killing, because that was most surely what the death was.

There was one other thing that snagged the eye and Juliet leaned closer, holding the flashlight as near as she could without risking touching the body or the walls of the crypt or tipping the stone lid onto Raphael.

The woman had a third nipple located on the side of her right breast. There was also a pile of clothing in the corner of the crypt. Juliet couldn't make out what all was there, but one garment looked like a sweater of fine wool and there were stockings—made of nylon probably. That was what they were making stockings out of in the fifties. Unless they were silk. Wealthy women had still worn them.

The corpse's polish on her nails—both fingers and toes—was perfect. Her hair was in a style that they had used to call a beehive and was an improbable shade of red. That likely meant hair dye or henna, but it could be part of the mummification process. It was not unheard of for corpses in South America and Asia to be found with red hair.

"Miss Henry," Bertram said, taking her arm and tugging her away. "It will not do for you to faint on top of the … body."

"I won't." She was touched that he thought she was so fragile. She thought about asking him to look at the nipple and confirm what she was seeing but recalled that his eyesight was failing. He was also looking rather pale and on the verge of being unwell. Juliet reminded herself that the average person would be something more than disconcerted at finding a body where it didn't belong.

"Bertram, I hate to ask this of you, but could you go upstairs and call the police? I'm afraid we won't get reception down here and I am feeling a little … overwhelmed. I need to sit for a moment." She added, "You might not want to say anything to the others just now. The police will not want the scene contaminated and you know that the curious ones will rush down to look at her. And someone will need to show the officers down when they arrive."

"Of course. I shall go straight away," he said gallantly and started for the stairs, clearly relieved to be away from the crypt and also to be handing the body over to the proper authorities.

Raphael looked at her quizzically as Bertram left and she remained standing at the side of the grave, but didn't ask her about the manufactured job she had sent their friend to do until his echoing steps were gone.

Juliet was about to say that she was relieved that at least this time the murder couldn't have anything to do with anybody in the house. But she

31

hesitated. Was that true? Certainly it was a remote chance that the fifty-year-old body had any connection to the artists who lived in other states and even other countries.

But what about the workmen who were finishing up the retrofit? She assumed that they were local and some might be old enough to have had some knowledge of the woman. And most of the staff—excepting Marigold—had been hired through a local agency.

And there was no saying that Marigold hadn't been to San Francisco before. She was too young to have personally had anything to do with the murder, but…. For some reason, she was thinking of Marigold as being part of the mess. Perhaps it was that both women had red hair, and the thought had crossed Juliet's mind more than once that if there was anyone in the house likely to end up as a corpse it was the temperamental cook who was so good at making enemies.

"Juliet?"

"I know that was manipulative," she said, answering the unasked question. "But there is no need to upset him by keeping him down here. Raphael, I'm sorry to ask it, but can you get close enough to look at the body's right breast?"

Raphael did not protest this odd request, but carefully maneuvered his chair to the other side of the sarcophagus and then pulled himself upright. Juliet shone her light on the nipple.

"Ah," he said. Then: "And she has red hair. Interesting."

"And there's the name on the marker. I think I read something about this in one of my old books about haunted San Francisco. This is the supposed witch's grave."

"You did read about it. I recall the story because you mentioned it being left out of the house's official bio. But I think it might be … instructive to ask Esteban to look a bit deeper into the details, yes? And he has an interest in such things." There was no distaste in his voice. He did not judge his friends for their interest in matters he did not find fascinating or even in good taste.

She looked at Raphael. His face was severe and pale. But it was always thus. And he was right that Esteban made a hobby of the morbid and would find the matter fascinating.

"Do you care? I know you are busy," she said, looking at his hands. They were beautiful and confident and capable of the most delicate work. They were not for shoving lids off of sarcophagi. Would the day come when he would get exasperated with her past and her ever present nature, which was to pry into the unexplained?

"Not particularly. She has been dead for a long time. But you do care and are bored, and it may help the police who are coming in rather late in the day—supposing they are open to assistance of course."

"Yes, always supposing," she said a touch gloomily. Police rarely wanted outside input.

"I hear Bertram. That was quite fast," Raphael said. "I think it would be best if we said nothing about this poor woman's oddities to him. It is not common knowledge, but he had two ancestors who were hanged for being witches. That is partly why he is so repelled by the very idea of being near a witch's grave. I doubt he would have come down here had he known of it."

Juliet winced.

"That's horrible. And I agree completely about keeping mum. De Smet wouldn't thank us if word of this got into the press after he had made an effort to suppress the details online."

"Good God," Raphael said. "I hadn't even thought about that. We must make every effort to keep this away from the reporters."

"Well, I'm thinking about it. Old habits." And she was. Not because scandal might ruin De Smet's Valentine's Ball, but because of the alarm bells that would go off in Washington once her name was linked to another notorious case. She could do without another extracurricular murder and the attention it would bring. Not that there would be any undue publicity about her. Merton would see to that. Publicity would ruin her usefulness to him. She would be ineffective if people recognized her at a glance as someone connected to crime on either side of the equation.

Juliet sighed. Her only permanent escape from the NSA would come with a bullet or a razor blade, or perhaps a comet striking the earth, and that seemed a bit extreme to avoid what was after all an annoyance. A huge one, to be sure, but not up there with world war and cancer.

Chapter Three

The crypt's stone angels looked on, mute witnesses to old events that had passed before the blind stone eyes and frozen lips. Perhaps they were supposed to be comforting to someone of medieval sensibilities, but Juliet found that she preferred the gargoyles on the outside of the house, which did not have human faces. They were dragonlike and had a purpose which she understood. The angels with their tiny teeth and mean eyes just confused her.

Juliet was thinking about the angels because she didn't want to give too much thought to other things. She believed in justice as some people did organized religion. But Juliet had come to a point in her life where she no longer wanted to be the instrument used by this particular god. It had never been part of her plan. She looked for patterns, helped ferret out truth from the chaos of misinformation. She did not want to spend any more time chasing down killers, however ancient, and her defense mechanisms were already rushing to the site of this new trauma and offering her distractions. Like her sketchbook. She liked sketching because it allowed her to think of nothing at all. Unfortunately, she could just imagine how the police would react to being drawn.

But questions remained while her hands were idle, the same ones she faced every time she faced proof of human mortality and evil. She asked herself what flaw in the killer's mind allowed him to murder, or if it was truly a flaw and not a proper reaction under the circumstances. Shouldn't anyone be expected to kill if they were threatened?

But why did she think that someone had been threatened? Was it because the body had ended up in a crypt made for a witch? Until she had answers, she didn't think that she could walk away.

Besides, the whole matter was intriguing if one kept away from the emotion of the event and didn't imagine the naked and vulnerable woman dying, not being able to grab one more breath as she tried to find a way past the belt around her neck.

Juliet did not believe in magic, either black or white, but she did believe in evil intent. That was the distinction that was made between murder and self-defense. So what were they looking at here? Was the killer someone who had come into the world with bad thoughts in his brain, or had life events put the bad thoughts there?

The woman's naked body made her think it was some sort of sexual murder. Naïve women were snack food for certain kinds of manipulators and predators of an even worse stripe. But there was that tattoo. The nipple she had added to her body suggested the possibility of other things besides naiveté.

And then there was the larger question of whether the killing had been a one-off or if the murderer had gone on to other darker deeds. The trappings did not suggest anything so mundane as the usual domestic disputes.

Old death was being overshadowed by the modern ritual of forensics. A techie began looking for organic trace evidence and another was dusting for prints. Juliet didn't think he would find much and what was in the way of DNA would have degraded over time, though the crypt was a good environment for the dead if preservation was the goal. Cool, pest-free, and dry in the airless vault. The stone however was rough and would not take prints. Perhaps on the belt....

The detective in charge was named Scanlon and he had eyes the color of dark rum. Like a dog. Only dogs didn't usually look that inquisitive so maybe he was more like a cat. In any event, Juliet was not at ease, though Scanlon seemed competent. So many of the police she had met lacked the proper imagination to build a decent case when the killer was anything but a violent spouse, or when there was a falling out among thieves who happened to be carrying guns. They had popsicle sticks instead of the iron girders needed to support original thought of the kind passing through her head.

From observation and listening to his questions, Juliet didn't think that rigid thinking was one of Scanlon's failings. But would he believe any deduction she shared—however accurate—was just a party trick, something thought up by a publicity-seeking kook? There were plenty of those around, especially when there was a sensational murder. Would he understand that she was adept at combing through the ether for facts, theories, and hunches that more often than not led to answers, even in cases where things looked impossible?

Especially then.

Another tech arrived and said something about the press.

Juliet didn't watch TV. A steady diet of so-called news caused people to live in a state of low-grade, constant fear that eroded happiness and beauty and hope—all things she found necessary to work. The fact that she knew most of the stories were at the very least distortions of the truth and quite often outright lies crafted by the oligarchs that owned the media—often at the behest of her old employer—only added to her disgust. She would never voluntarily aid the media circus.

That said, a part of her would be tempted to turn on the TV up in her room, concealed in a wardrobe, to discover how bad the publicity for this case was going to be. Once the details of the woman's physical condition and the location of her makeshift grave were revealed, the channels would be throbbing with speculation. They wouldn't be able to help themselves. As the old saying went: *if it bleeds, it leads*.

It didn't really matter, of course, what the media said. It wouldn't touch her directly. That did not mean that this event would leave her untouched though. Her fingerprints were once again working their way through the belly of the only beast that truly influenced her life. The detective would likely be told to leave her alone and that would make him curious, or hostile. Or both. And in return for this unasked for favor, her old employer would one day come calling and ask for her to do something for them in exchange for this consideration. Probably something dangerous and nasty since any dealings with them were a Faustian bargain. The fact that she was paranoid about the NSA was rather like a chronic illness, or maybe a recurring illness like malaria. In any event, the fact that she was chronically suspicious did not mean that she was wrong about probably hearing from her old employer in the coming days or weeks.

"You are well, Miss Henry?" Bertram asked Juliet, whose face was tight as she gnashed her teeth at the thought of dealing with her old Nemesis, which she found infinitely more distasteful than a dead body. Poor Bertram had been running his hands through his hair, which needed cutting and the reapplication of styling gel. The mussed tresses had him looking a bit like an unloved dog and she had to fight the urge to smooth them down.

"I'm feeling very old," Juliet said, unsticking her jaw and taking a sip of her coffee. She was glad that she had filled a thermos earlier so she had something warm for Raphael and Bertram to drink while they waited to be questioned. They had not been separated when the police arrived. There was no question of any of them being the killer and all they would be able to tell the detective was the circumstances of the body's discovery. Eventually. They were not the top priority while in the presence of the dead.

Bertram patted her hand. The gesture was awkward, but his sincere feelings were not.

"We all grow old—God willing—and wobbly in our frail anatomies which were not designed to last. Some nights we will lie awake at night listening to the disorder of our organs and unpredictable bowels. Those of us who had the blessing to find love and then suffered the horror of losing it will mourn the loss ever after. I have seen the world devastated by malicious lunatics—and fear I shall again. I have even had my honor trampled in the sewers of ignoble and petty minds who wished to destroy me because of what I am." He looked at Juliet under his beetling brows. "Well, so be it. We must go on regardless of the hardships we face. The only other choice is to lie down and die, and I do not choose that. And neither, Miss Henry, do you. That is not our way. It is not the way of any true artist. You must stay on and finish your work."

Juliet nodded, feeling Scanlon's eyes upon them. She did not say, since it would jar against his beautifully expressed sentiment, that it was not her art that she was worried about. It was the sword of Damocles that was ever poised over her head. Her past was something she had stepped into blindly when she was young and susceptible to flattery and appeals to her patriotism. But it turned out that she had not been working for the good of her country, and she had been trying with mixed success to wipe it off her shoe for the last several years. The thing about paranoia—once one had any proof of malice on the part of those around them—was one didn't know where to end it. There came a day when it was impossible to trust anyone. That day for her was long past and time had not healed this wound.

But that was a terribly selfish way to be looking at things when there was a woman lying dead not ten yards away. At least she would have an official wrapper, a file number if not a name.

Most people, herself included, lived on the surface of life, preferring not to know—or at least not admit—how deep the waters were beneath them. Because the water did accumulate drop by drop, tear by tear, and it stayed there, the disappointments, the pain, the grief, the rage of a lifetime. But Bertram *would* look from time to time and it would disturb him when he peered into the depths.

"Don't worry, Bertram. I am not giving up my work, nor would I abandon Raphael mid-project even if the police let me. What I am feeling is not so much horror at the fact that there has been a murder as, well, vexation," Juliet said in surprise and annoyance.

"Well, of course. This is not at all a common thing." And obviously he did not approve of unexpected bodies in the basement, even if it was a former crypt. "We are all much shocked and horrified by this."

"No—I mean yes, it is uncommon. It is just that I am surprised that the body is that of a stranger." When Bertram stared at her with consternation, Juliet clarified. "I was pretty sure it would be Marigold who ended up dead if anyone did, and the red hair rather threw me off for a moment or two."

Bertram snorted. He looked oddly relieved by her rather callous answer. Perhaps he had worried that she would cry or become hysterical.

"That one is definitely courting bad karma. Such an unpleasant woman. She must be brilliant in the kitchen for it is not her winning manners that endear her."

"Yes, and she also has red hair that nature never gave her. At least not at such an intensity. It's like she wears it as a ... badge. Or a declaration of war."

Both men looked at her, one puzzled and one speculative, but they said nothing more since the detective had finally joined them. Juliet was just as glad for the interruption because she wasn't sure how to explain her last comment. Her brain was snagged on that detail though, and that meant there was something important about this aspect of the situation that she did not yet understand. The idea had some strange curves and angles and she kept turning it this way and that, trying to get it to fit the pattern, but there were still too many other pieces missing. Eventually she would pick up enough strands to begin weaving a convincing narrative, but not yet.

Bertram patted her hand again.

Insufficient light can make things look magical. It can also make things eerie and unpleasant. The lack of light wasn't a problem for the police photographer who had a camera with a flash bright enough to give x-rays. Juliet closed her eyes against it and wondered at what point she should begin protesting their uncomfortable situation. A kind of temporal isolation was setting in. It had nothing to do with being alone. She was definitely not alone, but there were no windows, no clocks, no bells or chimes to mark the passing time. Appetite would have normally served as a marker, but for the moment she had been abandoned by the desire for food.

As expected, they were eventually asked for their names and addresses, and then they gave an account of finding the body. Mostly Juliet gave the account and it was brief. Scanlon was attentive to her answers but apparently not chomping at the bit to get the investigation started. He looked very tired and Juliet wondered when he had last slept.

He was also amenable to letting them leave the crypt once Juliet fetched a couple workmen to help with Raphael's chair. The detective was exhausted but still alert enough to realize that though he didn't want people tramping through a possible crime scene upstairs, or talking to the other people in the castle before he questioned them, it would not be a good decision to have outsiders there when they pried the corpse out of its box and tried to stuff it in a body bag. Letting them go was the lesser evil so he agreed to finish his questions upstairs.

Juliet did most of the talking once they were back in the living area and installed beside a fireplace in what they were calling the living room. Raphael was very pale—his normal state, but the detective didn't know that—and Bertram's accent was rather thick, especially when he was agitated. Scanlon seemed content for her to play spokesman for their group. He did not seem to think it odd that they would be down in the crypt looking at rather ugly angels and checking on the stability of a wobbly stone in a crypt that could be shaken loose in an earthquake. Maybe because no one had explained what it was they were restoring.

That casual interest could have been his laid-back nature or the results of a sleepless night, but Juliet didn't think so. Scanlon was calm and thorough, but again she thought more like a hunting cat than a good-natured dog. More likely this seeming acceptance of their story was from his being a detective in San Francisco where he had grown used to hearing about all kinds of odd activities among the colorful citizenry.

He was probably also wanting an interview with De Smet first, who might be assumed to have more knowledge of things like the house's history and the staff than artists brought in to do repairs.

Juliet wasn't holding her breath that his confidence would be rewarded with new knowledge from the owner, but didn't express her doubts. Better to let some things swim into the detective's ken when he was ready to hear them.

The detective did not object when Juliet asked if they might leave the house to have some lunch. When Scanlon hesitated, she explained that the screaming woman with red hair and wild cat-green eyes they had just *helped* upstairs was the cook and that lunch was likely to be very late if it appeared at all, he had checked his watch and then smiled wryly giving his permission for them to leave.

"Can we bring you or your men back anything?" she asked politely.

"Thank you, but no. I am pretty sure that there would be words if someone spilled mustard at the crime scene." Scanlon managed a second smile which was rather nice, but Juliet wasn't ready to get too cozy. His opinion of her might well change once he got her file. Or didn't get her file, which was more likely.

"The cook's name is Marigold?" he asked, consulting his notebook. Scanlon was old school and didn't use a tablet. "What is her last name? Is she local?"

"I don't know. She apparently amputated it," Juliet said. "And … she doesn't mingle a great deal with the artists on the project so we haven't had much opportunity to get to know her. She was also hired out of state, but I am not sure of where she has lived. She speaks French fluently."

Scanlon grunted.

"Is she always so…." He seemed to hunt for a word.

"Excitable?" Juliet hesitated. Marigold's reaction had been over the top, but she did have a habit of letting her emotions rule her. Still, Juliet had feared that they would have to resort to the traditional smack in the face to calm her down. Or, at the least, a smack of the brain with some kind of chemical either out of a bottle or from a syringe. "Yes, but it usually takes the form of angry criticism rather than screaming."

"Criticism of?"

"Everything. The staff mostly," Juliet said. "But, to be fair, seeing a body can be very upsetting. I need to be more charitable."

Juliet considered perhaps offering to check in on her but decided that that could be left for later. Raphael needed to eat and Bertram would do well to have some time away from the house.

"Yes, seeing a dead person can be upsetting," Scanlon said neutrally, probably thinking that the three of them were remarkably calm considering their discovery. "Even when it's a stranger."

"Yes, even then." But Juliet had heard the slight question mark and knew that he had also marked the red hair on both women. She wondered if he would have any better luck fitting that fact into the erratic pattern that had so far presented itself for inspection.

Juliet knew from experience that doubt was toxic. But so, too, was fear. She wasn't sure why she suddenly thought that Marigold might be afraid, but she did think it.

There were many things that might make a woman chronically fearful—an abusive ex was always a good suspect. But there were other things as well. If one were frightened of phantoms, there was comfort to be had in company. It was another matter if what you feared was real and perhaps hiding among those closest to you.

The important question, at least for Juliet, was whether Marigold's fear had anything specific to do with the old murder. She couldn't see how, given the age of the corpse and when the crime must have happened. And yet….

She would have to think about it.

Juliet noticed that afternoon when they returned to work that it did not feel like a house of sadness. Not even a house in chaos—or no more chaos than there had been because of the renovation—though there were still a few police about peering into corners and taking pictures of irrelevant things.

Juliet admitted that maybe the lack of grief wasn't so strange. No one had known the dead woman, they hadn't even seen her, and no one was worried that they would be tied to some stranger who had died half a century ago. They were also very busy and ready to get on with things without a lot of extra fuss. Perhaps because they had not seen the body, they were unable to imagine the violence done against it.

Except Marigold, and even she had rallied enough to phone downstairs and berate the window washer who had left streaks on her bedroom window. This had caused some eye rolling among the domestic staff, but no one was taking it very seriously since the beast was sticking to her lair and not allowing anyone admittance.

After lunch, while Raphael and Bertram returned to their tasks, Bertram murmuring happily over his tools which had finally arrived, Juliet checked her email and found a reply from Esteban. As per usual, he had been able to dig up all kinds of details on the medieval woman whose quasi-grave had been usurped by a newer corpse, scraped up from the dark corners of the Internet that most people never saw. The witch's biography made Juliet thoughtful, and she went about with a knitted brow while she made random sketches of Paul House that would probably not be useful as art, but which helped her think about the bits and pieces of information she had gathered regarding the murdered woman, or at least where her body had been buried.

Esteban had also confirmed her thoughts about the meaning of the third nipple. She could not think of a single innocent reason for the dead woman to have one. And the not so innocent explanations were rather sordid and alarming.

Chapter Four

"Miss Henry."

Juliet looked up from her sketchbook. The visit was not unexpected, but not really wanted either. There was a certain ironic consistency that when she met someone new in law enforcement it was almost always over a body. It was also often an ill omen of the relationship to follow.

"Detective Scanlon," she said pleasantly, noting that the detective looked rather more rested than he had at their last meeting. Lucky him; she was exhausted. Sleep had proven rather elusive though she had spent the night with Raphael who was usually a comfort. Too many nights in a strange bed had left her brain feeling as if it had been covered in dryer lint. "Were you able to locate Mr. De Smet?"

"We spoke last night. He is returning from New York this morning. He didn't seem to think that he would be able to be of much assistance to us though since he is not particularly acquainted with the staff. Not even his cook with one name though he asked that we be gentle with her."

This seemed to annoy Scanlon, though he made an effort to hide this.

"I guess good chefs are hard to find. The thing is … the very rich are…." Juliet stopped, wanting to defend De Smet but not being sure of how to explain him to someone as down to earth as Detective Scanlon. "De Smet has a lot of properties and strikes me as being a soul rather above such things as domestic management. He delegates and

hires those who are recommended. He isn't …
hands on with the day-to-day, small stuff.
Unfortunately," she added, thinking of the cook
who had forced her way into the crypt yesterday
afternoon, taken a look at the corpse, and then had
hysterics at the sight of the body. Juliet gathered
from talk around the house that morning that the
police had been completely disconcerted by her
unexpected arrival, had had to fetch the workmen
who had helped with Raphael to carry her upstairs
since she refused to move away from the body, and
they were wary of accusations of brutality if they
touched her. Juliet hoped the staff got bonus pay
since when she had been bodily removed Marigold
had been nasty and frantic, making any number of
threats against everyone who laid hands on her and
intimating that she would have them fired.

There had also been no meals the rest of the
day since the chef locked herself in her room and
refused to speak to anyone face to face, including
Juliet who had made a belated gesture of kindness
and been rebuffed for her efforts. If the house had
had a panic room, Juliet was pretty sure that
Marigold would still be in it, bossing everyone
around by phone or text messages.

Juliet just wondered if it was general hysteria
that locked the door to her bedroom, or if it was fear
of something in particular. It could be that finding
the body had touched on a nerve of some tragedy
past. Certain memories of her own were locked into
closets in Juliet's brain with signs on the doors so
she didn't run into them on accident while trying to
recall a quote from Shakespeare or the name of her

first grade teacher, but once in a while something happened and a door got opened by mistake. It could make a bad situation infinitely worse if old feelings were heaped on top of new ones.

"Yes, so I gathered. So, I've come bearing gifts to those who *will* talk to me."

Scanlon offered her one of the two coffees he was carrying. He studied her sketch of the gargoyle. It was one of the humorous ones that she planned to put on trick-or-treat bags and t-shirts.

"Thank you," she said, putting down her pad and taking the peace offering though she didn't especially want it. But she had survived bitter turf wars in the NSA where people tried to murder with bad coffee, so she supposed that she could endure takeout java in the interest of peace.

She noticed that Scanlon's hands were ringless. A lot of detectives she had met seemed to travel light. No wives, no families, no friends who weren't cops. To have lasted as long as he had, Scanlon had to have spent a lot of time looking into dark places. Probably he had gone through his emotions and thrown out those that didn't serve him. Others were locked up tight and only taken out on special occasions. He wasn't an emotionless jerk, but survival had dictated that he not be too empathetic with victims and witnesses. If he was to be *en rapport* with anyone, it would be the criminals he chased.

Juliet didn't blame him for this or for what was probably coming, though she would have to find out what mental calluses the detective had and work around them.

"This probably won't surprise you, but I made some routine inquiries about everyone at the scene and, quite unexpectedly, your report was by far the most interesting. Mostly because it wasn't in writing."

Juliet sighed, guessing what the next words would be and still annoyed by it.

"You had a phone call from Washington?" she guessed.

"Oh no. Don't be modest. You actually rate a personal visit. It seems that I am supposed to consider you above suspicion and—if I am wise—I will pay close attention to anything you deign to tell me about this case since you are 'a goddamned flensing knife when it comes to finding details.' In any event, we are not to annoy you with our investigation. In fact, I believe the exact quote was 'if Juliet Henry decides to screw the entire mayoral staff on the steps of city hall it had better not end up in any official reports.' "

Juliet was surprised into a short laugh.

"You must have spoken to Peter Davis. He has a certain inimitable style."

"No names were offered. The message was very direct and comprehensible though," Detective Scanlon agreed.

"And yet also offensive when it needn't be." Juliet took off the sipper lid since she wasn't three years old and tried the coffee. It wasn't bad. "Don't take it personally, Detective. I am retired NSA and I have *friends* in high places whether I want them or not."

Scanlon raised a shaggy brow.

"Are you sure about that? The retired part, I mean. My visitor didn't talk about you in the past tense. He seemed to think you were still part of the team and under the official shield."

"Oh yes, I'm certain about this. Never more so about anything in my life. Only since my boss also retired, I seem to be the only one left at the agency who acknowledges this fact. They want me back—at least for freelance—and this warning to you is their version of candy and flowers."

Juliet surprised herself by being forthcoming. Something about Scanlon made her feel at ease. She thought he would understand what her job had been like even if he didn't get her nonlinear thinking that sent her skulking down dark passages in her brain. He would know that it was almost impossible to be in the reactor core of intelligence work and not burn out. That she hadn't worked in a place where they had softball teams or Christmas parties. They didn't get together to drink on weekends and share their innermost secrets—mostly because those secrets were classified. How they all worked together, but there was no time for play, and friendships outside the office were discouraged. They were, in fact, encouraged to obfuscate their lives in case other divisions or agencies were looking on and wondering what the hell they were actually doing.

"And will you be going back to work anytime soon?" he asked. "If they ask very nicely."

"No. At least no more than I can help," she amended. "Their wooing can be rough when the carrot fails and they want something badly enough. Fortunately, the current division chief knows I don't respond well to threats of the stick and uses subtler forms of blackmail and coercion." And Merton seemed genuinely incapable of imagining that her *no* meant *not now and not ever*. Though he wasn't dumb enough to say so to her face.

"It sounds like a swell place to work."

"No, and the retirement benefits suck. But still I pray nightly for Merton's continued wellbeing since it seems best to deal with the devil I know and not the ones in other departments. You understand?"

Scanlon nodded.

"Would it be inappropriate to ask just what your line of work was that might make you of so much use to this investigation?"

"Officially, I made coffee and possibly screwed the boss. Unofficially … I began by tracking down sources of disinformation. This was back in the pre-Internet days of newspapers and magazines. I am good at pattern recognition and speak a few languages. Later this worked into steganography—that is unraveling hidden messages buried inside of media. And its opposite, burying messages in media to see who would bite at the lure. I also … I was kind of a trouble detector— radar that found people with ill will in their hearts. I was the boss's *secret* weapon. Only now, well, it's less secret than I would like."

"We all have our crosses to bear," he said, sounding sympathetic. "For instance, my boss feels that Mr. De Smet shouldn't be troubled by my investigation either. And Mr. De Smet in turn doesn't want his highly trained staff bothered. That probably includes you, but I thought I might talk to you anyway."

Juliet could imagine Scanlon's boss grinding his teeth as he got the call from the mayor or the governor suggesting that it would be a shame if De Smet, the generous and clearly innocent victim of a strange real estate transaction, was inconvenienced by this rather ancient matter. And knowing that it would be career suicide to express any other opinion. So he had had little choice but to pass the message on to his overworked detective.

Scanlon knew how things worked. He just didn't like it. All this interference from the outside meant that he would have to look for another way to be involved in the case, one not involving a frontal assault.

That was probably why he was talking to her in spite of the pressure from above to leave De Smet's people alone.

"That makes things a bit more complicated than usual," Scanlon added. "One might almost think that someone doesn't want this case solved though I really can't imagine why. Someone dead for fifty years can't have that much influence on people today."

That notion of obstruction hadn't occurred to Juliet. Why would they not want this case solved? Surely the detective was right that the roots of the case were so far in the past that the details couldn't matter to anyone except the family of the dead woman.

"I love a good conspiracy theory too, but I don't think anything is afoot here. This is just about the rich and famous being … *rich and famous*. I don't suppose the ME has reached any conclusions about the cause of death?" Juliet asked though the cause had looked pretty obvious to her.

Scanlon nodded, which surprised Juliet. Medical examiners almost always had to-do lists that didn't match up with the homicide detectives, especially when they didn't have a hot case with lots of media pressure. An old death would not be a high-priority item.

"Actually, this case rather caught the old trout's imagination for one reason or another, and he had a preliminary look-see straight away," Scanlon explained. "He says she was strangled *without elaboration.*"

"No sex or torture with the strangulation? No trophies taken?" Juliet asked then thought of the lack of purse and shoes. Had they been the trophy?

"Not that he can see after all this time. And as an aside, though her clothes were there, there were no undergarments, no shoes, and no purse. I'm assuming the killer took them, though they could have been removed by someone else any time in the last fifty years, so we can't count on it."

She nodded.

"So, you have straight-up murder though with some of the clothes missing from the corpse, which usually suggests sexual activity. Which probably can't be tested for after all this time. Certainly the DNA wouldn't have survived."

Scanlon shrugged.

"Usually it means that, but this time? Who knows?" He shrugged.

"Were there labels in the clothes left behind?" Juliet asked, recalling that her mother had had a couple of suits from a high-end boutique and that they had borne the name of the store rather than the designer.

Scanlon nodded.

"Yes, I Magnin. But they are long gone so there is no way to look at their records though that would have been a long shot anyway."

"In a way that's good. I guess. I Magnin started in Oakland and moved into San Francisco. I recall reading that the old store was burned after the oh-six quake. They also expanded into southern California, but not until the sixties. And they were very upscale. Someone who shopped there regularly would be noticed if they went missing. Or a tourist with that kind of money. She probably wasn't some prostitute who could fall through the cracks with no one noticing. That's a plus."

"Nor were there a rash of disappearances. At least not that were reported. But that still leaves a lot of names to check."

"But this is surely better than a psychopath or serial killer with multiple victims yet to discover. Um … you've opened the other crypts, haven't you?" Juliet asked.

"Yes and yes—and thank God they are empty. But as you probably know, a single murder is harder to investigate without a pattern of deaths to follow. Especially with very few clues to be found and so many years after an event. This will not be a walk in the park, especially if I have to do it on tippy-toes so the high and mighty are not disturbed." He was being very frank.

A bad cop—or a tired one—would be looking for a way out of this case, marking time before their retirement by not making waves. But someone still on top of their game would be looking for a way in. Be it through the paths of motive, evidence, or intuition. And it had to be that way especially when it was a case without any air left in its lungs and the usual methods had flat-lined, a case that couldn't be worked in the normal way.

Eventually, the endless procession of human-induced tragedies would wear Scanlon down, but hopefully not before he earned his pension. Today he was just annoyed at being thwarted in the chase.

"Yes. I don't doubt it will be a pain."

"So, is there anything you want to tell me about this case now that you've slept on it?" Scanlon asked politely. "I really feel that I need to ask this since I have been given such strong advice. And, though I wouldn't normally admit this, I think it might actually be good advice and I am not too proud to take it."

"Thank you. I think."

Certain theories looked silly by the light of day, but down in the crypt, in the presence of the murdered, they had been obvious enough to make an impression. And conjecture and theory were what led one out of the maze of bewildering possibilities when actual evidence was thin on the ground. Juliet decided to walk toward the rabbit hole and see if Scanlon balked at the edge. Given the pressure on him, she thought it possible that he would be willing to at least peer into the dark.

"There is one thing that struck me, in particular. You saw that the body had been tattooed with a third nipple?"

"It wasn't a birthmark or a mole?" he asked. "The exam was preliminary and the medical examiner hasn't finished his report. Tox reports will also be a low priority. Not sure when it will be done. It's an old death. I don't think anyone is putting on a full-court press when it comes to paperwork and won't unless the press gets heated up about it. So far, they have been distracted with that whale washing up on the beach but we can't expect to remain that lucky."

Juliet shook her head at his warning but didn't disagree with his assessment. From her point of view, the less press the better, though she was sorry for the whale.

"No, it was not a birthmark or mole, nor was it a natural nipple, though it sometimes happens." She looked at him, wanting to see how he was taking this theoretically complex bit of information. She thought she recognized in him a fellow observer who used intuition's peripheral vision to peer around corners without committing to an entire train of possibly misleading thought. That he didn't flee at the onset of her presentation was a good sign.

"Weird. What do you think it means?" His voice was neutral. He wasn't rejecting anything, just reserving judgment on something that was likely to sound odd.

"This choice of body art could have just been some bizarre but meaningless affectation, of course. I knew a man in his seventies who had himself deliberately scarred so he looked like he had been beaten with a bullwhip. There are some bent people who like to do strange things to their bodies. But there were no piercings that I saw and no other ink on the body. Whoever she was, she wasn't a hardcore modification freak."

She looked at Scanlon, giving him the chance to contradict her. When he didn't speak right away she added, "Sometimes tattoos like that are used to identify members of a *grotto*."

"A grotto?"

"Yes, it means a group composed of people within geographical proximity, but usually clandestine in nature." Some spy networks were organized that way. "The tattoos are identifiers, more subtle than secret handshakes. They are used when members need a way to sort out who belongs to their subsection or clique when they don't know each other by sight. One might be able to do it with clothing or jewelry, like a Mason's ring, but that would be fairly obvious to any decent observer and there are occasions when clothing would be unhelpful. Like at a swimming pool or the beach."

He grunted.

"But an extra nipple? You couldn't exactly flash that on a streetcar or in the grocery store."

"No, it would be a way of identifying others during a certain kind of ceremony. Where there weren't clothes or people all carrying copies of the

New York Times or whatever other sign they would normally use to introduce themselves."

"I see." The voice was still neutral.

"There was nothing else on her body, was there? No other hidden brands or markings?"

"Nope, nothing that I saw at least."

"I find that highly suggestive and rather unpleasant. Especially given the woman's hair. Did you catch that? The style is right out of the fifties—that helped to date her time of death—but it was also probably dyed or at least *enhanced*. Women weren't as into body adornment as they are these days. Hair dye wasn't that common, especially nothing that bold unless you were in Hollywood or a streetwalker. A tattoo of any kind would have been rare as would that shade of hair. I don't think she was your average housewife."

The detective nodded, peering down the hole where she had led him and squinting as he looked for her point.

"The hair was dyed. Why does this bother you especially?" Scanlon asked. "The red hair, I mean. Maybe she just liked Lucille Ball. Though I guess the nipple is kind of peculiar too given the era of our Jane Doe. There weren't as many cults back then. Not for women anyway."

Our. Well, maybe the murder did sort of belong to her. It came with finding the body. Juliet took the first step into the tunnel leading into the dark madness of her theory. She didn't try to enlighten him about just how many cults had been available for women back then. They had been called "clubs" and "societies," but they had had

62

recognizable cult trappings and in many cases were quite pernicious.

"Eras are a handy way of thinking about things, especially for people who came after them. Kind of like general statistics of an age. But history is rarely as cut and dried as history books make it seem, especially not when applied to a particular case. For instance, people talk about pre-Vietnam and post-Vietnam and there were cultural and political changes that eventually happened, of course, but most of the attitudes and habits remained unaltered for many years. People still went to church, looked for true love, tried to get rich. Some people wanted to change the world and made themselves stand out so they could be seen and maybe make their messages heard. Others were just as anxious to get their way, but they chose to blend in, burrowing safely into society and working in the dark. Most of what was going on—in any era—never made it into history books even as an obscure footnote."

"Agreed."

"And there is a habit of thinking that people in the past were more naïve or innocent or unsophisticated because they lacked technology or education or didn't share our linked-in online culture, but they really weren't any of those things. Don't think that it was all like *Leave It to Beaver* and *The Ed Sullivan Show*. There is a darkness in certain people then and now."

"You're saying that there were people even in the fifties who knew about recruiting for their causes and cults, and there were always people who were anxious to join them. Even women who wore gloves and funny little hats and shopped at Union Square."

"Yes. And some of those causes were evil. At least by most people's standards. And the leaders of these cults would have been very charismatic so they could persuade people to their ideas. Society as a whole just wasn't always aware of them because these subversives weren't trying to be Joan of Arc or Rasputin. Or Elvis. These cult leaders knew it was best to keep a low profile and recruit carefully. They would have had followers who were willing to do anything they asked. They always do."

She thought of De Smet briefly but decided not to use him as an example. Scanlon wouldn't understand until he had met the Belgian himself.

"Okay, I'm with you. The fifties had Charles Mansons too."

"Good. Now, if you climbed into the way, way back machine where many of the ideas for cults began, you would find that the church—the Catholic Church and its inquisitors—believed that a third nipple was a sign that a witch or warlock had been suckling demons. They were also not partial to red hair and considered it a mark of the devil. It got many women burned. And it wasn't just in European culture that auburn hair marked you. Red hair in China was thought to be the mark of a vampire. Choosing red hair *could be* a way of making a statement against an institution or a cultural bias. An act of defiance. Or a token of loyalty to someone or some cause."

Scanlon stared at her over his coffee cup.

"Sorry, that was kind of a hard left. So you think this woman was a witch? Or, more likely, someone thought she was a witch? Or a vampire?" He shook his head. "I can't see it. I actually know some witches. They're harmless—very new-age pagan. Lots of vegans and crystal wearing. Not the kind to bring down a murderer on themselves. And I don't see her as the kind who hung out in Chinatown, so I think we can rule out the vampire angle."

"No, I don't think she was a vampire or a witch—at least not a Wiccan. That is what most modern witches are and probably what you are thinking of. Wicca is a religion, and as religions go it is pretty harmless though some worship skyclad—nude," she explained. "That would be a good place for wanting some kind of identifier like a tattoo. And even in the fifties it wouldn't have been that alarming—not in San Francisco. But I think she may have been involved in something else a bit seedier. A regular witch would not tattoo herself with a third nipple. Some other sign maybe, but not a nipple."

"Okay, so what was it then? Some sort of sex for the great goddess, religious prostitution thing? Maybe white slavery? Or like that book. What was it called? *The Story of O*?"

"I doubt she had anything to do with *nature* worship with sex. The manicured finger and toenails, the over-groomed hair which is pretty short. And the *leather* belt around her throat—a ladies belt, you will have noted, so probably her

65

own. Of course, those things aren't a positive bar to worship of an Earth goddess. But…."

"But?"

Juliet shrugged and committed herself to her theory.

"I think she might have had some connection with, or perhaps even actively practiced, devil worship. That went on the in the nineteen fifties too," she added when he looked surprised. "And in Europe, the nipple tattoo was fairly common among adherents of certain sects. It still is."

The shaggy brows moved again. Juliet didn't bother to explain that she had learned about this in one of her old cases at the NSA or that Esteban had confirmed it with his research. She also did not show him the drawing she had made of the victim.

"So she was a foreigner after all? Maybe a tourist?"

She hated to ruin his moment of hope.

"Maybe, or a resident. But it is just as likely one initiated in a European belief system. They exported it everywhere. It is also suggestive that her body was concealed in that particular crypt," Juliet added.

"Why?"

"Do you read Latin?" Juliet asked him.

"No. Somehow I was absent on days when the academy was teaching dead languages."

"Well, I wasn't. That crypt doesn't read like the others down there that all have the standard *here lies so and so, beloved daughter blah blah gone to the angels*. This one asked for prayers for the soul of Sancia Perez Reverte and promised good karma

66

to those who were willing to do it—a sort of discount on sin, layaway of future Divine favors type of thing for those who would say a rosary for her. Basically, someone was trying to buy the poor woman a way out of hell." Or so Esteban believed. They had talked again before breakfast, and he had emailed her an image of the one portrait said to be of the condemned witch that was above and beyond what she had requested. Juliet had a feeling that he was intrigued and might very well end up taking a vacation in San Francisco if work permitted.

Scanlon digested this as he stared at something in his own memory.

"Reverte. That's a Spanish name, isn't it? For some reason that rings a bell, I wonder if there is a local connection and that's why the old guy bought that grave...."

"Yes, it is a Spanish name. And, yes, there were a lot of Spanish in California because of the missionaries and being part of Mexico. But the grave is older than that by a century or two and I don't think the woman—the one we found in it yesterday—was Hispanic anyway."

"Fourteen forty-eight was the date," he said, proving he had a good memory. "But I thought I read in the paper that this castle was Dutch. Why would a Spanish woman have a grave here? Was she married to a Dutchman or something?"

"Grave *marker*. Not an actual tomb to house a body. It was too small to hold even a small woman if she were laid out in the regular manner which is why the corpse was folded in sideways. There are no bodies down there in the crypt—or there

67

shouldn't be. They were supposedly all reinterred in other cemeteries when the building was moved. And the house is actually made from the parts of three ruined castles which are Dutch, French, and from the Valladolid province of Spain." Scanlon stared. She thought it was out of interest more than surprise. Little surprised him. "The first owner of Paul House bought up ruins of churches and castles and art from all over Europe and fitted them together like a jigsaw puzzle, using the extra bits for the wall in the garden. It's sort of a mini Hearst Castle in that way. This isn't just one house. It is many. It is why the architecture isn't entirely harmonious in certain sections."

"And the part from Spain is the grave marker of a … what? A witch? A devil worshipper?" There was definite distaste there. "And someone else knew about this and chose the grave on purpose?"

"Well, there were several things that could get you in trouble back in the bad old days. They burned people for being goblins and werewolves, believe it or not. By that time summoning storms and demons got you more than a few days' fast and some Hail Marys, though they used to be more lenient about that. But mostly you got tossed on the fire for being a witch or a heretic. In those days, they did not make much distinction between being a mere witch or midwife and being a minion of Satan. Or a heretic. To them, it was all the same and the victim was damned to Hell regardless. According to a friend of mine who is really good at research, Sancia Perez Reverte was both a heretic and a witch and possibly an adulteress as well. She supposedly gave herself, body and soul to the devil for unhuman knowledge of how to kill her wealthy husband with some unknown disease or poison which afflicted him after he returned home from a visit to Rome. And she died for it when she was twenty-four. She was strangled and then burned. They were being merciful because she confessed under questioning and her brother was an important man in Spain and forked over a lot of money to the church which they were reluctant to give up. The grave is just a memorial. She would never have been buried in it—not even her ashes, assuming they could sort them out from everything else that was burned that day."

"I see. I guess. Poor thing."

But a woman executed centuries ago wasn't his problem. Or hers either.

"Probably. Unless she did poison her husband," Juliet said fairly. "I gather that he was kind of an asshole and not very nice to the people who worked for him. The question I have been asking myself since we found the body was why this other woman was killed and stuffed in her grave. There were other larger crypts nearby that would have better accommodated the body. Was the killer someone with some pretty esoteric knowledge?"

Scanlon pondered this idea and then surprised Juliet by saying, "Okay. I'll accept all this. And I can see what the poor thing might get out of selling her soul, but why would the devil want to buy it? Did they ever say, or did the why of it just not matter to the bastards who killed her?"

"You are looking for logic in her inquisitors? Some modern notion that one needed a motive as well as means in order to convince the jury?" She shook her head. "Or are you speaking of *our* dead woman? Maybe we should call her Jane for now."

"Sure, why not her—Jane—though I was thinking of the first one too. A body, that I could see wanting if she were pretty or smart enough to be useful in some way. But what is a soul worth really? Especially a woman's soul since, if I recall my feminist history lessons, they didn't seem to think that they were valued much as people."

It was Juliet's turn to think about this. The seemingly pointless question began to gain traction as she thought about it. She had been considering what would cause someone to murder the red-haired woman in the crypt, not so much about the original inhabitant who was also—by Juliet's own modern standards of belief—murdered through ignorance and even malice. But might they not have some other relationship to each other? The question felt like one that should be asked. But was there a connection beyond the obvious one of both women probably being considered witches and ending up dead because of it?

Had they been innocent witches, persecuted for their religion? Or were they both something worse?

Could the killer have chosen that grave because it was already unhallowed or deconsecrated and therefore a suitable place for an unclean body while the other larger crypts were not?

That suggested a murderer with an unusual view of the world and one who knew the house's history. Perhaps a former owner? Or someone who had worked there at the time of the killing and was sufficiently interested in architectural antiquity to enquire about the history of the grave markers?

Scanlon was waiting. Juliet made herself focus on his question. He was obviously also feeling the connection between the two deaths but having a hard time making any logical ties between two women murdered centuries apart. Sometimes ideas could not be approached head on, but rather required some elliptical reasoning. Juliet decided to try it his way.

"The soul—as the Catholics understood it then and I guess still now—refers to the innermost aspect of a person, that which was divinely made and therefore of the most value and more important than the gross flesh created by procreation," she said slowly. "Not that flesh wasn't important. After all, feudalism was in full swing and they needed bodies to work the fields and the mines of the overlords and fill the churches at mass," she added. "And even women had souls with value, though it was a very near thing and the bishops only decided it because an Irish priest came down in favor of the idea."

"Yeah? So I guess they cared back then if someone sold it because it gave them some kind of power and they might start rocking the boat and wanting regular meals and stuff like that. Maybe trying to influence their husbands." He swallowed more coffee as he cogitated. "But in the nineteen fifties? With cars and electricity and antibiotics? Why would people care then about some ignorant person who may be selling their soul for a little bit of clout? Everyone would know it was just symbolic. Science was the actual power. Technology. Atom bombs. People didn't truly believe in witches and magic anymore, did they? They had surely stopped believing souls were for sale and would have thought the woman was mental if she tried to auction it off."

Juliet shook her head in contradiction of this statement.

"No. I wish—but no. And it isn't just an isolated crazy or two who believed in Satan. Look at the Temple of Seth headquartered here in the city. Also, the Church of Satan started here—though that is actually more about hedonism than classic worship of the Christian devil with black masses and so forth. I'll concede that *most* people had stopped believing in witches and magic by nineteen fifty—which is understandable. I think seeing Nazis at work changed our definition of evil and made us stop thinking of biblical or magical Evil, the kind with a capital E engineered by a supernatural Satanic mastermind, and made us see that there was plenty of evil lurking in the minds of twisted men. That was in part why the last witchcraft laws were repealed in England back in the fifties. But there was a woman convicted of witchcraft around that time in Omaha and banished from the community for using dark arts, and there was another put on trial in Pennsylvania for being a witch, so the idea hadn't totally died out in rural areas. And then there is New Orleans with its own kind of human carnival of freakish behavior. Belief is alive and well down there at least in certain quarters."

Scanlon grunted but made a note in his old-fashioned black notebook.

"New Orleans maybe. But in San Francisco?" he asked again. "I can see kids pretending to believe in the devil for kicks and giggles when they got bored with smoking dope and dropping acid. But believing that junk enough to murder someone? Besides, I haven't ever heard of the department having problems with these groups. At least not since I joined. We get our share of whack nuts, but they aren't organized."

The more he argued against it, the more certain Juliet became that she was right about her theory.

"Why not here? Not everyone is an enlightened native and not every person stopped believing in magic when we got electric lights—even today there are people who believe absolutely in the Devil—and someone who truly believed that Satan's handmaiden existed, not as a misguided pagan who liked dancing naked in the moonlight and selling herbs and potions at flea markets on the weekend, not even as a neo-feminist encouraging other women to get uppity through goddess worship—but someone who had actively renounced God's most precious gift and sold their soul to Satan for gain that they might have the power to harm others—like causing plagues or hurricanes or other holocausts as some were accused of doing—they might very well kill the suspected witch if they had the chance. And they would do it without remorse because, without the soul, the body is just flesh and no longer human. That isn't murder. Especially not if the killer believed they were being the Lord's agent. And they would consider it to be a public service to kill such an abomination before she could cause harm—or further harm—to her victims. Especially if they were also dropping acid, though I am not sure that was going on much in the fifties, was it?"

Scanlon nodded and Juliet realized that he had already worked this out. That he had figured it out so quickly impressed her. Usually, the police were resistant to "weird" ideas.

"So, you're saying that I'm probably looking for a crazy who believed in the Devil and thought this woman in the crypt was an evil witch—a Satanist."

"So, you *could be* looking for someone who thought they or their family were being harmed by magic of any flavor. I am thinking Satan but wouldn't rule out anything just yet. Whether they were actually being harmed in some way is beside the point since obviously it needn't be this particular devil's quisling who plagued them with whatever misfortune or disease that led the killer to murder as self-defense. In fact, it probably wasn't the woman's fault. At least, they were not actually harmed in any magical manner, no matter what she might have said or done to anyone. But if the killer already believed in Evil with a capital E, they would just need suspicion of some supernatural event and a sign that this woman was God's enemy and was filled with the malicious intent to harm them," she added. "I know that sounds nuts and I wouldn't rush to put it in any reports just yet, but I'd say it's at least plausible."

"Plausible."

"Yes. After all, what would *you* do if you truly thought you were being persecuted by a Satanist who successfully practiced black magic, knowing that the law, and the rest of society for that matter, would never believe you if you accused her? And even if they did believe you, that you would still have no legal legs to stand on if you tried to sue or have her arrested? Me? If I feared for my life, I'd probably kill the witch," Juliet said. "*If* I truly believed that and thought I or my family was in danger. It would be wrong—crazy even. But I would probably do it. And given that I am organized, I might very well find a convenient place to dump the body before I acted."

There was silence for a moment and then Scanlon shrugged off the tension.

"Yeah, after my early visitor and I chatted for a while, I kind of figured you would feel that way," he said with the ghost of a smile. "It's good that you are too enlightened for that kind of nonsense. Because thinking that someone was actually able to use magic is crazy."

"As a loon," she agreed.

Juliet wasn't flattered by Davis's reading of her character, even if the assessment was accurate, but did not let her annoyance show.

"Of course. It could just be that someone committed a murder down there for some other reason and opened the closest grave to hide the body," Juliet pointed out. "Maybe it *was* kinky sex gone wrong—the woman changing her mind about doing it when she saw the graves, and pissing off someone with a last minute refusal to fornicate on a crypt. I may be reading things incorrectly because of where the body was hidden, giving the killer too much credit for having what he thought were supernatural but righteous motivations for killing something evil." She paused. "I do wish that they had found her shoes though. Or a purse. It might have given us an identity and also some clue about who the killer—or the woman—was."

The detective stared. Juliet wasn't offended. He was thinking rather than being rude.

"Yeah. My dad used to have his shoes made by a cobbler. Went to the same guy until he died. If the shoes or purse were handmade locally or they were something really exotic that only a high-end store would sell there could—maybe—be some kind of record still sitting in a back room or basement."

"Maybe. It's a long shot, but there had to be some reason he took them away instead of leaving them in the grave. Or maybe they were borrowed from someone…." Juliet suggested. "Something that had to be returned to their owner or the woman would be reported missing right away. Maybe taking her things was about buying time before she was reported missing, and not taking trophies, or hiding her identity."

It was Scanlon's turn to think. "That's good. And taking her to the crypt to kill her … Maybe it could be that the killer was looking for a good shot at an insanity plea if he—or she—got caught offing the inconvenient wife or girlfriend. That would be tidy," Scanlon said, apparently enjoying the intellectual exercise.

Juliet supposed that she could forgive him that. The murder was old and the chances of his solving it were probably slim. This was a cold, cold case and taking him away from more urgent crimes that needed attention. But De Smet, being a man of importance, was being given the best treatment and attention for this little problem in the basement.

"If that's it then the field of suspects is pretty narrow—maybe psychologists and lawyers. I don't think the average Joe would think that way. Unless he had a lot of imagination and a very cool head. Especially for the time. Remember, they didn't have police shows on TV back then. And it would still have to be someone with access to the house—even if no one was living in it at the time. It sure would help to have a more definite date of death to work with. An empty house could mean that she was killed anywhere and just dumped here. If it were occupied then the list of potential killers and opportunities would shorten."

Scanlon nodded and finished his coffee.

"I'm off to look at dusty files on missing persons. This will take some time because the oldest records haven't been computerized yet. There is also a very real chance that the killer is already dead and so I am completely wasting my time. But mine is not to reason why." He paused. "You know, Miss Henry, in another era, they might have burnt you too."

She nodded, acknowledging his point. She might have been thought a witch and a heretic and just too damned smart for anyone's good.

"I shall pray for you in your hour of need," Juliet said.

"Thank you, but I am not sure that that will do me any good though. If you aren't a believer in good standing."

"Who says I don't believe? And it depends on who I pray to, doesn't it? Maybe the old gods listen."

"Point taken."

Scanlon tipped her an imaginary hat and Juliet went back to her drawing.

Her mind wasn't focused on the rather average gargoyle she was sketching and after a while she decided that maybe she needed a walk. Perhaps it was time to visit the Temple of Seth or the Church of Satan and see if they could help her find if someone—oh, say her mother—had ever been a member back in the fifties when she suddenly disappeared. Surely they would be interested in a possible new recruit. All churches were. Unless it was more a business than a cult. She was sure that it was a business in some respects, even if a nonprofit. Organizations always were when the IRS was watching. That meant keeping records.

Chapter Five

In some instances, one could be hindered by a surfeit of information. Too many leads, too many confused witnesses. Too many suspects. In this case, it was a dearth of known facts that troubled Juliet. That was when imagination and fortitude were most required.

Walking the undulating pavement made Juliet very aware of the fragility of the bones in her feet. This wasn't a city designed for strolling in thin leather soles. She should have changed shoes though the dainty flats rather matched the role she had in mind to play. Her whole outfit was slightly impractical and overly feminine, assembled out of bits and pieces from her duffel. She hoped that it visually lowered her perceived IQ and made her look more innocent, or at least like a housewife rather than a professional investigator. She didn't want her intelligence to protrude because it tended to bother people.

Experience had taught her that the truth was most likely to be found when sought in person and without advance warning which would allow people to invent excuses not to see her or think of plausible lies to her questions.

Juliet paused outside the open gates and looked around. The tourists were all around her like a flock of birds—wool-coated crows and quiet wrens, but mostly macaws in sweatshirts proclaiming all the places they had visited. All of them seemed to be hunting for shiny objects to collect while they ate and drank their way across the town, many wearing earbuds that pushed chosen sounds into their heads. A few of them had the confused look of a UFO abductee dropped off in a place they didn't know and weren't entirely sure that they liked. The general smell of the crowd was of coffee, hot dogs, and marijuana. It wasn't a bad combination on a cold day. The pigeons thought so too and darted among the passing feet in reckless pursuit of dropped crumbs.

But crowded as the sidewalks were, none of the chattering crowds came too close to the wrought-iron gates. They were not especially formidable. There was no sign saying *abandon all hope ye who enter here*, but the pedestrians seemed to sense this wasn't a place where tourists were welcome. No one came here by accident thinking they might find an ice cream parlor or a jewelry store or the local mahjong parlor or porn palace. Though it did have a shortage of windows and those that existed were placed too high for anyone to peer in casually.

Even the birds stayed on the boundary laid out by the iron fence. The starlings and pigeons chattered among themselves but did not venture into the enclosure.

The exterior of the Temple of Satan was not aesthetically pleasing being rather non-specific and painted an off-putting gray and black color scheme, but at least the abstract art at the entrance was not grotesque. The dark stone statue could be Death, but it could equally be a skinny orca. Those not up on their Egyptian deities might even mistake it for some kind of hooded saint.

Nor were the old cedars snugged against the fence necessarily threatening. Unless one knew that they were often used in cemeteries and temples where people worshiped the dead.

Juliet snorted.

No, the building with its deeply pitted stucco would not be mistaken for a business office, a retail store, or a daycare, however much it had the same kind of generic, mass-produced, strip-mall feel. Juliet thought for a moment and then she had it. The temple looked like one of those funeral parlors from the fifties which were so often abstracts of a conventional church. They used a lot of cedars in their landscaping too.

Juliet noted the days and times of worship posted on the wooden sign in the azalea bush surrounded by a cement walkway embedded with white quartz that would be blinding on a sunny day. It all seemed rather conventional and normal though clinging to a look that should have been let go a few decades ago. The building wasn't dusty or faded or ill-kept, it seemed a bit like a crotchety old man squatting on a bench in a rundown park. There was no need to be nervous. The place was just dated and with its true purpose turned inward rather than on outward display for the public. Again, much like a funeral parlor.

Juliet glanced at her watch, which was on her right wrist, her tracker being buckled to her left. She looked not because she had an appointment or that there was an appropriate hour for calling on the would-be damned, but because she was suddenly missing Raphael and hoping she would be back to

Paul House in time to have lunch with him. Normally he would have been with her on this sort of adventure—and would have been had she asked him—but he was very busy and up against a deadline which he would hate to miss. She had decided that she would not distract him from his work simply because she was bored and felt the impulse to help Detective Scanlon with his sleuthing.

Her phone rang and she answered when she saw who was calling.

"What's up?" she asked.

"*Bella*, you sound breathless. What are you doing?" Esteban asked. "You have been standing still for rather a long time if you were walking for the benefit of your health."

Bella meant beautiful. It was what he always called her though she was not sure why. He was also monitoring her via her tracker. Theoretically he shouldn't be able to do that, but Esteban could do almost anything with computers.

"I am standing outside the Temple of Seth. It's actually kind of ordinary looking for a den of iniquity. I can't really believe that they sacrifice babies or devour the entrails of virgins here."

There was a short silence. Esteban had done enough research for her that he didn't need to ask why she was at the Temple of Seth.

"And are you planning to depart with wise haste, or seeking admittance to this less than delightful locale?"

"Seeking. Actually, I am looking for my long lost mother who joined up in the fifties."

"Ah. I can guess why, of course. But you will call me when you are done? I should like to know the state of your body and soul."

"Of course," she promised, feeling better. "I don't think I'll be long. This is a Hail Mary anyway."

"But your Hail Marys often receive answers. Sometimes bad ones. *Ciao* for now, *Bella*, but call me soon so I may be at ease."

"I will," she promised and meant it.

Feeling braver for having some support even if it was long distance, Juliet walked into the dark courtyard and up to the tall double doors that seemed to be the only means of entrance to the somber building. She pulled open the heavy doors—they were fire code compliant and opened outward—and found herself in a small foyer with gray indoor-outdoor carpet that reminded her of a hotel lobby from the seventies. It also had the same silence as a hotel and that suggested heavy soundproofing.

She did not check on the threshold, but her first breath gave her pause. It felt like the air had been trapped since 1958 and didn't have enough oxygen. Perhaps it had passed through too many lungs, some of them diseased.

There was also a feeling of vacancy, that there weren't enough bodies to fill up the place. There were no echoes. Those were swallowed, smothered even. But the quiet was that of abandonment.

Juliet let her eyes adjust to the dim light. She was surprised to discover that there was someone at the oak desk under a stained glass window that was heavy on the red tones, perching in a large leather chair that resembled a throne. So the building was not completely abandoned.

At first she couldn't tell the aged creature's gender but the nameplate said Spiros, so she went with the idea that he was male.

Juliet had heard it said that some old people had hands that looked like bird claws but had never actually seen this before. She also couldn't entirely suppress the feeling that she was looking at a turkey because he had a definite wattle. There wasn't a patch of visible skin that was not wrinkled or mottled.

It was hard for her not to believe that his chosen religion had deformed him, though probably it had nothing to do with the darkness of his spirit and everything to do with unfortunate DNA or even an accident.

"Hello," she said softly, doubting if there was anyone else in the building. "I wonder if you can help me. Or direct me to someone who might be able to help."

"I shall try," the pleasant voice coming out of the wasted body replied. The eyes were dark, so black that she wondered if they were contacts. They studied her impersonally but thoroughly. "What is it you seek?"

Juliet, who had been ready to express a desire to get to know the King of Hell just like dear old Mom, decided that she would try something a bit more believable for a fifty-something woman who was feeling rather nervous.

"I believe that my mother was a member …
here. Back in the fifties. I was hoping…." Juliet
trailed off and allowed her face to show some
distress. It wasn't hard. The place, while not overtly
awful, still had an unpleasant taint and lighting that
belonged in an old Frankenstein movie. Perhaps it
was the smell of the air which was still as anything
in Paul House but less healthful and it truly felt
depleted of oxygen. Could that have been
deliberate? An aid to helping members hallucinate?

Or was it something worse? She had heard of
places back in the sixties that had piped inhalants
through their ventilation systems. Could she be
smelling the remains of some drug?

"My mother … she left my father when I was
very young. She wasn't … she wasn't happy at
home. My father was a very … strict man. Very
traditional. Religious. It was only after he passed
that I found some of her things and found out just
how bad their marriage really was. There was a
letter with her diary from a friend suggesting she
come to San Francisco. To come here, in fact. And I
wondered if there was some way…." Juliet faltered.
"You see, she just disappeared. For a while, she
would write to her sister but then there was nothing.
The last letter was in nineteen fifty-nine. Anyhow, I
was just wondering if maybe there was someone
here who might have known her, who could maybe
tell me something about her. Maybe someone who
would know where she went?"

The wrinkled face showed no skepticism, but
then it couldn't show much of anything.

"Very few of our members have been here that long. I only joined in nineteen sixty-eight."

"Oh." She allowed her disappointment to show.

"There are some records though. Will you come with me to the office?" he asked, rising. "What was your mother's name?"

She marveled that it was going to be that easy. Juliet thought fast, reviewing plausible fifties names and chose the name of her friend at Bartholomew's Woods who was about the right age.

"Rose Montgomery—that was her married name. Her maiden name was Reed. But I don't think she would have used either one. I think she wouldn't have wanted my father to be able to find her." Juliet looked away as though ashamed to admit that her father had been a wife beater.

"And the friend who wrote to her? What was her name?"

"It was hard to make out. The letter was old and the writing was not very steady. It was also just one name." Juliet took a chance. In most of the cults she had known, single names were preferred when people baptized—or whatever they did at a Satanist's temple—into a new identity. "It might have been Hexy or Hezy. Something with an H."

"Well, let's see what we have."

"Thank you."

The floor, though carpeted, creaked as they walked over it, making Juliet wonder if there was a basement. Thinking of what might be in it was rather a cause for anxiety. Sacrificial altars? Hooded robes and other diabolic vestments? It seemed unlikely that it was kindhearted grannies knitting socks for homeless orphans.

The office looked exactly like something in a funeral home down to the box of tissues on the desk. The only odd note was a statue of the Egyptian god Seth, standing in a narrow wall niche, lit by a red light. There was a desk with a computer and behind that a bookcase with a collection of leather books and folios. It was all very tidy. Apparently the damned didn't care for chaos in the office however much they might seek it in the wider world.

"When I was little, I always liked Seth best. We had a book in the library that showed the Egyptian deities," Juliet confided, for the first time telling the truth. "The other gods looked silly to me, but I liked Seth. And Anubis. He was pretty good too."

She thought she saw the thin lips twitch. The ledger he removed from the shelf and opened on the desk was old but in fair shape. Juliet came closer, but not enough to seem intrusive. The pages had yellowed though Juliet suspected that the pages were parchment rather than paper. He did not offer to show it to her but the writing was bold and she was able to read upside down.

"We were very few in number in the beginning," he said. "And there were not as many ladies with us as we have today."

Juliet suspected that there hadn't been any *ladies* with them, but of course didn't say this.

"Interesting," he said, tapping a name with a yellowed finger.

Juliet nodded encouragingly though she wanted to shake him for being cryptic and coy.

"We did have a member named Hesiod. But it seems she left us in nineteen fifty-eight."

Juliet could see the other name by his finger. It was Francie Allen. The amount of money beside her name was impressive for the era if it was a weekly tithe.

He didn't volunteer Hesiod's other name though it was right in front of him and Juliet didn't press. Most of the members of this group probably preferred to keep their association private, which she could understand.

"Was there anyone else who left then? Maybe my mother went somewhere with her friend. Does it say where they went—maybe to another branch of the chur—temple?"

"We were the founding branch in the US in the fifties. I am afraid there was no other until late in the sixties and that was in New York."

"Oh." It wasn't hard to sound disappointed again.

"We seem to have lost two other lady members around that time."

Juliet followed his finger down the page, reading quickly as it paused.

"But there were a couple other members who left around that time. One was called Davina." *Margaret Hogg*, Juliet read. She hadn't been as financially generous as Francie Allen. "And the other was … Carin."

Rose Dean, *grotto, anger's blessing* the ledger said, and Juliet thought he was shaken by it. She was too. Of course, *grotto* could mean anything. It didn't prove that she was part of some special subgroup of the church. It was suggestive though.

She hoped that Spiros was also convinced of her story. The choice of names had been fortunate. Uncannily so. That might lead him to take a special interest in her and she preferred that he and anyone else he talked to think her harmless.

"There were no addresses for them?" she asked hopefully. "No … I don't know. Nothing that could help me find my mother?"

"I am so sorry," he said, closing the ledger and starting to rise.

Juliet would have liked a longer look at their records, but she supposed that Scanlon could arrange to have the records subpoenaed if it was necessary.

Or perhaps not. She wasn't sure about the conventions regarding religious records, even if they pertained to fiscal matters or a murder investigation.

Feeling that the carrot was always better than the stick, Juliet decided to leave on a high note in case she needed to return for more information.

"I am not sure if this is appropriate," she said, "but I wonder if I might make a small donation. I appreciate your help and since it seems like maybe my mother was here…."

"Why thank you, Miss…?"

"Mrs. Henry," she said, deciding to be somewhat truthful in case he somehow tracked her down. She reached into her purse and pulled out a twenty-dollar bill and offered it tentatively.

He took the money gently, not showing if he thought her donation too little.

"I will add it to the holiday fund. We are planning to be part of the interfaith Christmas display this year." He spoke without irony.

Juliet forced herself to smile politely and nod. Actually the idea amused her and she wondered what sort of display it would be. A baby demon in the manger? Seth in a Santa hat? Would they have all red lights? All black ones?

"Thank you again for your time," she said, also rising. The ebony god seemed to be watching her from his place on the wall.

"Good luck with your search," Spiros said. He didn't offer to pray for her.

"Thank you," Juliet said again, looking away from the statue and moving toward the door. Suddenly the room seemed unendurable and she longed for fresh air.

She also wanted to write down the names before she forgot them. It wasn't much to go on, but it was a start. She hoped Scanlon was grateful and efficient, and that she didn't need to return to the temple. Juliet wasn't superstitious, but something about the place made her flesh creep.

Chapter Six

"Miss Henry?" Scanlon asked politely, waiting to be invited to take a seat on the ledge where she was perched, sketching one of the most difficult to access gargoyles that was tucked on the far side of a turret. She was questioning whether it was worth the effort.

Juliet was feeling better after her lunch with Raphael and second phone call with Esteban, whose arrival would be delayed since he was helping a client who had wandered into a whole lot of trouble at the border.

"Detective, what joy?" she asked, turning carefully to look at him.

"None, alas. We have candidates for our Jane Doe—several of them. Dozens even. And that is just in San Francisco. It seems that the fifties was a popular time for women to pick up and move without leaving a forwarding address. Even among the foreigners. Few were thoughtful enough to have fingerprints on record. And the consulate is not sounding hopeful of finding anything else after all this time. Discovering Jane's identity may take a very long time."

Juliet snorted and closed her sketchbook, easing herself into a more comfortable position on the ledge. She gestured to Scanlon to take a seat on a nearby bench.

"It may be that I can help with that. As it happens, I went to visit the Temple of Seth today."

There was a pause.

"Indeed. And how is his infernal majesty?"

"Oh, I didn't get to see the head man himself since I didn't have an appointment. I did see the secretary though, a man called Spiros, and he was very helpful in assisting me to look for information about my mother, who happened to be a member of the congregation back in the fifties. Especially after I made a small donation to their holiday fund. I hadn't realized that they had one, but they do. I looked it up."

Scanlon raised a brow. She thought he was amused. That was better than annoyed at her interference.

"They decorate in public these days— especially in the Bible belt, or so my researcher friend says. It's a freedom of speech thing. I actually feel kind of okay about contributing to that," Juliet confessed. "Maybe I really am a bad person."

"I see ... and was your mother actually a member of the Temple back in the fifties?" Scanlon asked, looking absolutely fascinated.

"Heaven forefend. Mother was a devout Methodist. I lied. I figured that it was in a good cause and it is okay since the church's head man is supposed to be the father of lies. At least, I think Seth is just a sort of a ... visual distraction from their real creed, which is mainstream Satanism as described by the Christian adversary." Juliet pulled her small notebook out of her pocket and flipped it open to the last page which she tore out. "Here are the names of three congregants who left without any word to the church officials. An effort was made to find them, I think because they had money which they tithed—or whatever it is they do—to the temple. Sorry. I don't have anything except names—there were no addresses, ages, or details about hair color in the ledger. And, by the way, it wasn't kept in blood. I was a little disappointed about that. I thought maybe they would be old school about that."

"I'm not disappointed," he said dryly, taking the list.

"But think of the possibilities of matching DNA. I think the last name on the list is probably the most interesting."

Scanlon looked at the three names. Francie Allen (Hesiod), Margaret Hogg (Davina), and Rose Dean (Carin—grotto, anger's blessing).

"Thank you. I will check them against the missing person reports. This could shorten the search by a whole lot and heaven only knows when I would have gotten around to visiting there. Believe it or not, I've managed to avoid the place so far." He smiled a bit as he folded the paper and tucked it into his coat pocket.

Juliet nodded, resisting the urge to point out that Rose Dean seemed to be associated with a grotto. Scanlon had eyes. He would act on the information or not. Pointing out the obvious would probably only annoy him, and that would be a shame since they were getting on so well.

"Any thoughts about the why of things?" he asked.

"Yes, but they are just thoughts."

"I'm all ears. I don't have any scenarios that make sense or play better than any others."

"Shakespeare once said that 'men have died from time to time and worms have eaten them, but not for love.' " Scanlon's brow went up. "That is probably true. But it's different for most women. I think the killer murdered her because he was frightened of her. But I think she may have gotten herself killed because she thought she was in love."

"Really?"

"It's just a thought. I can make the scenario play that way. It doesn't help with finding out who she is though. And we have to accept that we may never know the why of it, or who killed her."

Scanlon nodded once.

"So, I Googled you, Miss Henry. Couldn't figure out why you were here. Still can't. You don't do restoration work, do you, not like the others? Or are you painting something original for the house?"

"Lord, no. I'm not famous enough. And my style is all wrong for Paul House anyway. I do t-shirts mostly. I am here because of Raphael James. We are ... involved and my being here makes things easier for him."

"But you have sold a few paintings—and for a good price," Scanlon said. "You are a real artist."

"Yes, enough to make my living at it anyway. I've had a few biggies that were picked up. There is one in a private home in Tahoe, one in a gallery in Napa, and one in the home of a Nazi war criminal in Mexico. I did okay at the modern art show."

"You sold a painting to a Nazi war criminal?" Scanlon asked.

"To the war criminal's son. It was sort of my price of admission to get into a very prestigious art show I was ordered to attend."

"I didn't read about that one."

"No. It wasn't that kind of art show. I was doing one of my reluctant favors for my old employer, tracking down a piece of art that had gone missing in World War Two. I must say, it was decent of him to pay for the painting when he could have taken it in trade for the *objet d'art* that I needed. Or just murdered me," Juliet added. "I'm sure the thought crossed his mind."

"But he liked you too much to kill you?" Scanlon guessed.

"He liked me. But I also showed him where there was a stash of Incan treasure on his land and pointed out that the NSA would be back, probably *en force*, if he didn't give me what they wanted."

"And he was a reasonable man when the argument was framed that way?"

"He was very reasonable. When required. Unlike his father. But the old man is dead now so let sleeping Nazis lie."

Scanlon shook his head and got to his feet.

"I noticed that you wear a personal tracker. Do you like it?" he asked, changing the subject.

"Yes, oddly enough I do. It is a present from Raphael, though at the urging of a mutual friend who I think wanted to experiment with the limits of monitoring. Usually I am not fond of electronic leashes, but this is rather fun. And at the end of the day I can complain to Raphael that I have had to climb eight dozen flights of stairs and he feels obliged to take me out to dinner someplace nice."

It also had a GPS so she could be found in an emergency. Esteban knew how. She wasn't expecting to ever need it since she didn't hike in the wilds, but she hoped she would never need automobile insurance either. It was just nice to know that it was there in case something happened.

"And he doesn't mind the reminder that he can't climb stairs with you?" Scanlon asked seriously. "I think that might get to me."

"Nope. This may be hard for a mere mortal to understand, but Raphael James has been touched by God. The truly great do not indulge in things like self-pity. They are too focused on their art."

Scanlon shook his head again.

"It must be nice to be so confident. So engaged in one's work."

"I've often thought so," Juliet agreed.

"Maybe I'll stop in and see how the job is progressing. I don't get to meet the God-touched that often in my line of work."

"Me either. Go see Bertram as well. He is another one that got way more artistic talent than any human deserves." Juliet decided to add one more thing. "And try to be patient with De Smet. I think he is also on the side of the angels even if he doesn't always act like it."

Chapter Seven

Juliet ran into Marigold on the main stairs. They stood to one side so that there was room for the workmen to carry up the cleaned tapestries that had just arrived. Marcus Trent followed them, acting like a nervous dog. He paused in his unneeded monologue of advice long enough to give Juliet and Marigold a hard stare.

Juliet supposed she couldn't blame him. The crying and hysteria of the previous two days had stopped, but Marigold's face looked slightly inflated and as incapable of expression as a pink balloon. The whites of her eyes were bloodshot and made the pupils look very green. She had made an effort to hide the ravages of emotion, but the blotches of blush only emphasized how puffy she was. Her nerves were also disturbingly near the surface and annoying to Juliet, who nearly winced in sympathy as the cook flinched at the arrival of every person—actually, it was every man—in her personal space. Her seeming over-reaction to the previous day's events was worrying and suspicious, though what she was to be suspected of was still an unanswered question.

"How are you feeling?" Juliet asked as the men pushed by. Marigold had doused herself in her favorite perfume and she smelled like toilet bowl cleaner.

"Awful," the woman answered truthfully and touched the pendant at her throat. Juliet was surprised to note that it was not a religious medallion, but appeared to be a pair of elaborate letters entwined with serpents around some kind of stake, perhaps a caduceus. Before she could get a better look, Marigold had tucked it away. "But Mr. De Smet will be here for dinner and I can't disappoint him."

Juliet nodded, trying to appear sympathetic while she kept her breathing shallow.

"I would offer to help but I am afraid my skills end at tuna sandwiches and iced tea."

Marigold shook her head, either in refusal of the notion that she might need help or at the hopelessness of Juliet's culinary skills.

"No, you go do … whatever you do. I'll handle the kitchen and those slack-wits who are supposed to help with the serving and cleanup. Honestly, can no one follow instructions?"

Grief or fear or whatever she was feeling hadn't made the condescending cook any more pleasant to be with so Juliet just smiled and continued down the stairs, ignoring that the other woman was frightened to the back of her eyes. One could offer help but not force people to accept it.

And enough was enough. She adored Raphael, but Juliet was beginning to feel that leaving Paul House would be a very good thing for all of them. Hopefully, he would be finished soon and they could go home until the Valentine's Ball.

Taking Marigold's advice, Juliet went off to find some more gargoyles and cherubs to sketch, though her book was already bulging and she was heartily sick of mythical creatures. She supposed if the monsters proved too elusive she could always go and watch Bertram or Raphael at work, though that might be annoying for them.

She needed to do something. She felt antsy and her skin was crawling the way it sometimes did before a big storm. She had a rare urge to seek out the comfort of another mammal, but few besides her cat could be at ease when she was prowling and testing her mental dowsing rods on her theories.

As she wandered with her sketchpad and pencils Juliet thought about the dead woman—Rose Dean? It was irresponsible to start thinking of her that way, but Juliet's imagination had already decided that this was a fact. Arguing with it was futile until there was contradictory evidence.

Juliet tried to imagine what had happened the night—or day—that Rose died. The wolves of thought kept circling, looking for some new theory they could flush out or even attack. Juliet didn't try to call them in. It wouldn't have done any good once they started prowling.

The body was not bruised or scratched. She had not fought her killer. Had he held a gun to her while he walked her downstairs and made her take off her clothes?

Or was it first love that lured her to her end? Or a casual pick-up with someone exciting? The crypt seemed like the place to take a goodtime girl looking for a perverse thrill, which she could very well have been.

But a woman who had just discovered the new beating of her heart that came with first love would also follow her lover there, wouldn't she?

Could someone who worshipped Satan fall in love? Was it that much of a biological imperative?

Either way, Juliet wondered, had the killer had guileless eyes when he led her to her death? Or had she been blinded by emotion and maybe drink, and not looking carefully at the man who would kill her, therefore missing what must surely have been lurking deep down in his gaze?

The time and place were certainly perfect for the killer. Was the house empty because of careful planning on his part, or had it been a dare from the gods of opportunity that he could not refuse?

Was she—could she be—a sacrifice? The strangulation fit that scenario.

Of course, it fit others just as well.

Or did he see his opportunity to take her life as a sign from the one true God—whichever version he followed—that he should act at the moment provided by Divine providence? Most likely he was a believer in some version of the Christian God—because without belief in God there would have been no certainty in the existence of Satan and therefore less motivation to kill for one's beliefs.

She supposed it didn't matter anymore whether he was meticulous or just lucky, a true believer or an atheist psychopath. He had killed and a woman was dead.

It only mattered if there were more bodies to find, more murders to solve so that families could quit wondering what had happened to their kin. And fifty years on, even that would not be an urgent matter for most people. There was no reason to feel so on edge at being thwarted.

Juliet opened her sketchpad and stared at a large candelabra. It could be pretty done in oils with the small fires shedding their light on the glossy wood table.

But even as she drew, her mind went back to the tragedy and she ran through all her scenarios again. It had become a splinter in her brain, irritating her even when she worked.

Experience had taught her that some people were just bundles of violent paranoia and hatred swaddled into a deceptive human wrapper. She had known a few people like this and there was always the same anger and insanity staring out of their eyes, and their thoughts were always tied in knots around ideas and self-justifications that made sense only to them. It was this sameness, more than any religious dogma she had ever heard espoused, that made her almost believe in the idea of a unified, universal, and orchestrated evil. And the hard part was knowing that no amount of therapy would help them past their sick beliefs, nor any amount of prison time reform them from this inborn propensity to violence. They were evil—born evil and they would die evil.

If they were animals instead of humans they would be put down immediately for the good of everyone around them, but because these creatures had opposable thumbs they were treated as being worth saving.

She hoped that the killer had simply been paranoid. That was sad enough, but it might mean that he had never killed again and that there weren't more people wondering what had happened to

Grandma or Great-Aunt Gertrude. Maybe he had been a misfit who couldn't get a date and hadn't passed on his disease to anyone else.

Hopefully, he was long dead.

Juliet felt as much as heard someone walk by the archway that led into the dining room. She spun quickly and caught a glimpse of Addison Smith heading toward the kitchen. He was wearing a knit cap and a scarf wrapped several times around his neck. She hadn't noticed it before, but he smelled faintly of cigarette smoke.

Juliet frowned, wondering if she should intercept him. Today was not the day to test Marigold's limits, which the man from the historical society seemed to do rather more easily than anyone else.

But she was distracted from this goal by a blindfolded muse on the left side of the fireplace whose lips seemed to suddenly smile in the flickering light of vines scratching against the window. Unlike her companion who was looking out into the room and sneering at the gluttons who came to dine there, the other muse had her head bent down and a hand outstretched as though seeking her way past the fireplace.

It was not the excellence of the carving or even the rather odd theme that gave Juliet pause. It was the way the finger-wide shaft of light pushing through the velvet drapes was illuminating the seam between the muse and the frame around the giant firebox. In time, even with excellent care, wood will dry out and shrink. Joins and seams become loose and visible. So do panels, even ones that were oiled regularly and built to be kept secret.

Juliet set down her sketchbook and walked over to the fireplace. She began feeling along the join between the muse and the mantle. Her body blocked the sun which had alerted her to the slight gap. Since sight would not aid her, she closed her eyes, letting her fingers tell her when there was a change.

It took her a moment, but her hands found what she sought. There was a latch behind the blindfold. She pushed and prodded gently and was rewarded with the statue swinging open, its base moving on some kind of roller which made everything work in silence.

Juliet did not enter the space right away. Instead, she went to the window and opened the heavy drapes, letting in more sun. Most tales of booby-traps in castles are just that—tales, usually invented by some screenwriter or desperate novelist to add word count or cheap thrills to an otherwise boring story. But not always. She had been in a castle in Italy where the traps in the castle itself, as well as the garden, were very real. Caution was therefore in order.

However, what she had found inside the narrow opening was not some secret stairway, nor a priest hole, nor a forbidden wizard's laboratory where he had been making monsters or potions. It might once have been one of those things but now it was a panic room with a cot, a desk, a laptop, a fine selection of wine and canned goods, and also a small display of firearms mounted on the wall on old iron hooks that had probably held tongs and cooking implements.

Juliet almost snorted at her disappointment. So, she had been wrong about De Smet. He was not insanely brave or naïve going about without a bodyguard except when being chauffeured. She was ready to bet that he had a bolt-hole on every floor which she could probably find if she were willing to hunt for them.

Juliet stepped back and closed the door carefully and then put the drapes back the way they had been.

She felt a bit deflated and at a loss about what to do. She had been hoping to make some extraordinary architectural find that she could share with De Smet. Instead, she had found the mundane.

Juliet picked up her sketchbook and wondered if she could visit Raphael without annoying him. Or perhaps she should pay a visit to other institutions of damnation.

But no, she was certain that she had discovered the victim's identity already. It was Rose Dean. There was no need to do more laps around the block.

Her phone rang and Juliet answered it with relief.

"*Bella*?" Esteban's voice was faint and she walked toward the window. Reception in Paul House was spotty.

"Hi. I was just thinking of doing something pointless and maybe dangerous and wishing you were here to talk me out of it," she said.

"And what did you decide?"

"That it would be pointless and dangerous. But I have to tell you that I am very bored and also feeling … edgy. I would worry that this is about the murder, but how can it be? The killer, even if he were still alive, would probably be in a wheelchair by now. I must just be picking up on the other ghosts which are bound to be haunting this place."

"I don't know why you are feeling fey, *Bella*, but I hope that you will control your wilder impulses until tomorrow. I should be able to get away by later tonight and I will join you in your pointless and dangerous activities tomorrow if you like."

"Thanks," she said, meaning it. "I could stand being around someone who wasn't so caught up in things. I think I've gotten too close."

"Your voice is faint. A pity your phone does not have the strength of your tracker."

Esteban's voice was also fading.

"You can see me even in the castle? I didn't blink out when I was in the panic room?"

"I can always see you. I just can't always hear you."

"I guess I should have sprung for the model with the Skype feature. Except they don't have one."

"They'll probably have one for Christmas." She could barely hear him.

"See you tomorrow," she said.

"*Ciao, Bella.*"

Chapter Eight

"You are very restless tonight," Raphael said, looking up from the book he was reading. They had discussed her discovery of the panic room, but Juliet decided not to make him listen to her three-hundredth iteration of what the killer might have been thinking when he decided to kill his victim.

"Yes. I think I may have to go down and raid Alain's library. And maybe the kitchen. I would love a cup of hot chocolate. I could bring you one if you liked."

That was the usual bromide for sleeplessness.

"Thank you, but no. Shall I wait up for you?" he asked.

"No. Go to bed if you get tired. I may try and walk off some of my jitters. I don't think I have my full ten thousand steps for the day."

"Very well. Have a care in the dark."

"I will."

The castle had electric lights, but Juliet opted not to set the house ablaze. She did not want company as she tried to walk off her uneasiness. Because she was uneasy. There was no logical reason for it, but something had her nerves on end, their antennae out, searching for the slightest vibration that would mean trouble.

And of course, they found it.

As had been said before, as ye seek so shall ye find. The first alarm was nothing terribly obvious. Just the sound of a small gasp and the stringency of lavender, just a whiff that overlaid the ghosts of dinner which lingered near the kitchen where Juliet was pacing. There was no reason that the scent shouldn't be there. Marigold might very well have some important reason to be in the kitchen. Alone. Late at night. And she could have seen a mouse or been shocked to find a smudge of mustard on an appliance. If that was the case, Juliet would as soon leave her alone.

But was her presence in the kitchen likely, given her lingering fear?

Perhaps, if she believed that it would give her a chance to do something in safety while the rest of the castle slept.

But what could that possibly be? If it was related to meal preparation surely she would make her assistant come down with her.

Juliet hesitated, uncertain about whether to keep on toward the library or to detour to the kitchen. She could take a quick look and then get back to the library.

Should she turn on the lights, announcing that she was there, and hopefully avoid sending Marigold into hysterics? That would be the normal thing to do.

Something kept her hand from the switch. Perhaps because whoever else was abroad in the night had decided that they wished to move in darkness. *Because*, the thought intruded, *it might not be just her and Marigold moving in the dark.*

And what if someone else was awake? What did that matter? There had been a murder in the castle, but that was decades ago.

Except … it did matter. Every nerve in her body said that danger was nearby. She did not know where and did not know why, but it was close.

Juliet shut off her small light and turned from the library. Feeling her way along the corridor to the kitchen with her fingers, she hunted after the traces of pungent floral.

She halted at the open door which led down into the crypt. Even without the faint light from the pocket flashlight she turned back on, she would have known where she stood. The welling up of cold chilled her body and soul. This was where the scent was strongest.

Could Marigold actually be down there instead of in the kitchen? But why would she go there in the middle of the night? For that matter, why—as terrified as she was—would she go there at all? It was the place most calculated to terrify someone.

The smell of lavender lingered in the air. The voice, the small gasp she had heard had been Marigold's, she was sure. The memory of it hovered in the air.

She didn't want to go down to the crypt even if Marigold was there.

Juliet felt a stab of guilt. She had disliked the cook enough to resist the idea of Bo Peeping her through her nerves though she had been frightened since the discovery of the body and perhaps even before. And now something bad was happening. At the very least, Marigold was trying to find something, alone and frightened.

Or maybe she wasn't alone. Maybe she had decided to trust someone with her secrets and she had chosen badly.

Another smell. Kind of like mothballs and old ashtrays.

Juliet felt the hair on her arms and neck rise.

Damn it. She knew that smell and knew who it was down there with the chef. And they would not be having a romantic tryst.

She did not know why it was that he was there, though at a guess Marigold knew the reason. And had known or at least suspected and had been using herself as bait and had been caught.

Juliet peered into the dark, debating whether to announce herself and to check that something was truly amiss and try to deter whatever was happening by forcing the awareness that there was a witness.

She heard her old instructor telling her to stop being an idiot.

Juliet began to listen with her right ear, turning her head slowly to the darkness. The right ear sent its messages to the left brain where it began to process the information logically and swiftly. Nothing definite. The acoustics were odd down there and her own heart was very loud though she was careful to control her breathing.

Lights flared below.

There were no more sounds from Marigold. Neither of the visitors was inclined toward conversation.

Did he have a gun? He might. Clearly he was reluctant to use it if he did, but that didn't mean he couldn't be frightened into action if he were startled. But what....

Fortunately, she smelled the would-be killer before she saw him—or he saw her—and turned off her tiny flashlight, flattening herself beside the door. She needed to do that anyway so that her eyes could adjust to the dark and also not give her presence away should the killer decide to check more thoroughly on his privacy before getting down to work.

Juliet stood in silence at the top of the stairs but remained off to one side so she would not be backlit. She looked down at the lighter square in the darkness that was the entrance to the crypts. She watched until his head appeared, perhaps sensing her, peering up into the darkness from the top of the stairs and breathing hard enough that she could hear his laboring lungs. Carrying an unconscious body was hard work. Marigold should be grateful that he had not simply rolled her down the stone stairs. That he hadn't done that suggested she was still alive and that some part of him understood what he was doing and was perhaps appalled by it.

So, she hadn't imagined anything. Death had been stalking the castle all along.

Once the danger had revealed itself, Juliet was calm and able to think clearly. There was no time to summon help in person since everyone was on the third and fourth floors, and there was almost no chance that her cell would have a signal down in the belly of the castle anyway. Her plan to save Marigold was hastily erected and she had to hope the scaffolding would hold.

Her body was awash with epinephrine and glucose and adrenaline, all readying her mind and body for action. Later she would feel sick as the chemicals ebbed away, but at the moment she was strong.

She descended the stair lined with the gilded angels who grinned idiotically overhead, listening carefully, muscles ready to leap or roll or pounce— or flee. Though running upstairs from a man who might be armed was not the first choice she would make. It would be better to face him and fight.

She moved carefully, the voice of her old instructor, Jessop Carmody, in her head: *Remain invisible, inaudible, unfindable until in position to strike. Do not reveal yourself unless confident of success in your attack.*

Juliet had never thought that she would care to be haunted, but Jessop's ghost was welcome company as she inched down the cold stone treads.

Juliet had been prepared for a lot of things, but not to find an unconscious Marigold's head in a noose and angel Gabriel being used as a makeshift gallows as Addison Smith tried to haul the woman's comatose body into the air.

Not waiting to come up with a more detailed plan or shouting any warning, Juliet launched herself at him, hitting him in the stomach and knocking him backward into a sarcophagus. He dropped the rope as he fell and Marigold collapsed on the floor. She wasn't moving, but Juliet's first worry was the killer who was snarling at her. He could not move quickly though because her blow had temporarily paralyzed his diaphragm and stopped his breath.

Juliet was pretty sure that Jessop was smiling down at her.

Now finish him.

"Don't move," she warned him, not wanting to kill him but realizing she might have to.

"Evil woman," he gasped, either at her or at Marigold, as he managed a breath of air.

"Maybe, but you stay there. I would rather not—"

The first jolt was hard. The floor shifted sideways. Only a few inches but it threw Juliet off balance.

She had been in earthquakes before and recognized the thunderous stampede for what it was. But her previous quakes had been gentle rollers. This one wasn't. Two sides of the fault had finally slipped and torn part of the earth in different directions.

One of the guardian angels toppled down from its perch and barely missed her head. Juliet did her best to get to Marigold and to drag her closer to the nearest crypt, which offered the only possible shelter if the roof gave way. It had taken her a long and agonizing moment to free the chef from the noose since her left arm was numb from the blow she had dealt Addison Smith.

A moment later the frescos over the stair gave way, blocking up the stairs with golden body parts and broken mirror. A wall of aerosolized plaster rolled into the room.

The lights lasted just long enough to see Addison Smith still leaning against the tomb by the stairs get half-buried under falling cement and plaster. One of the cherubic angels crushed the left side of his head and he fell to the floor and then the world went black.

The cannonade continued, loud enough that Juliet did not hear herself cry out when something hit her shoulder. Dust filled the air, choking her.

She wanted to reach for her flashlight in her sweater pocket but she feared that she might drop it, so she rode out the stampede of dragons in darkness, clinging to Marigold and doing her best to shield her though she wasn't certain that the chef was alive.

Stone fell around them, but eventually the noise and shaking stopped.

Juliet finally fumbled for her flashlight, her other arm across her mouth and nose trying to filter the dust out of the air before it clogged her lungs.

The narrow beam showed that the damage to the crypt's angelic sculptures was complete. The shattered angels lay broken on the floor. But the walls of the crypt were intact as was the ceiling. Nor had any crypts opened. This was not the call to resurrection which would open every grave.

Had her situation been less dangerous, Juliet might have wept with relief. As it was, she turned her attention to Marigold when the woman began to moan and then cough. Juliet reassured her and looked her over as best she could and could find no injury beyond severe bruising at the throat. It was difficult to be sure though because they were both covered in dust and the light was poor.

Feeling obligated to check, Juliet worked her way over to the blocked stair and had a look at Addison Smith. The man was dead, there could be no doubt. Half his head was pulp. The other half was what caught her attention. He had two pupils in one dusty eye. Then she realized what she was seeing. Addison Smith had been wearing contacts, hiding the fact that he had the same weird green eyes as Marigold.

"Ah," she said, and the puzzle pieces began to come together.

The plaster and cement shifted on the stairs and Juliet jumped back, fearing that there would be an aftershock and further cave-ins, but it was just rubble settling.

They were safe for the time being, but how long would it last? How long would it be before anyone thought to search the crypts for them? Had the castle collapsed completely burying them in tons of rubble? Would people assume that they had been crushed in their beds?

And what of Raphael? And Bertram? And everyone else in the house?

"Stop it," she scolded herself and returned to Marigold. The light was not bright, but she could see that the dust was already settling. The room was large. They would not run out of air for a long time. The castle had come through the '06 quake and Loma Prieta shaker without falling down. There was no need to panic—in fact there were a whole lot of good reasons not to give in to hysteria.

She pulled Marigold's head into her lap and then turned out the flashlight.

The chef whimpered at the returning dark, but Juliet explained that they might need the light later if they had to find their way out.

"Okay," Marigold whispered, beginning to shiver.

"If you can, tell me about your mother," Juliet said to the trembling woman as she did her best to wrap her arms around her and keep her warm.

"You know about her?"

"Some of it," Juliet said.

Though it had to hurt her, Marigold began to talk.

Chapter Nine

Juliet, Bertram, Esteban, and Raphael were dining in the private suite at the hotel where Alain had insisted on installing them for what remained of the night and for the foreseeable future. He owned the hotel and it had suffered no damage in the earthquake. Neither had the rest of Paul House, at least nothing major that was apparent to the eye, but it would need to be inspected before anyone moved back in.

Juliet was betting that inspection would happen quickly since the Valentine's Ball was coming up and there was still work to be done to make it ready.

They had retrieved their clothes from their rooms at the castle before vacating and were able to shower and dress, but Juliet was exhausted and none of them had any urge to appear in public before dawn. Fortunately, room service was very happy to accommodate them.

Juliet knew she owed Esteban a huge debt. Because of the fitness tracker and the program on his phone he was able to tell the rescuers that Juliet was definitely down in the crypt, and she and Marigold had been found and dug out after only a couple of hours.

At first she had been uncertain if she was hearing digging on what used to be the stairs. The sound had been faint, the scratching of a rat or the shifting of the house as it shuddered in shock at the assault.

Marigold had fallen into sleep or fainted and Juliet had not tried to wake her. If the crypt was

117

about to come down on them there was no need to make her face the horror. Uncertain if she wanted to see death coming, she had hesitated a moment before switching on her light, but in the end the need to push back the darkest black she had ever known was overwhelming.

It was good that she did that. The rescuers had seen her light through cracks in the rubble and that had spurred them to greater efforts to clear the stairs. Soon she had heard voices, among them Esteban's.

Juliet did not weep easily, but the tears came then leaving tracks in the dust on her face. She hadn't realized how demented she looked until she saw herself in the hotel mirror. The only upside to her horrific display was that there was no way that any of the journalists or cameramen at the scene could have recognized her.

The rescue crew had brought two stretchers and they were both needed. One for the living and one for the dead. Juliet had walked out under her own steam, moving quickly in spite of pulled muscles. She had been on the verge of a second round of tears when she saw Bertram and Raphael waiting for her, both of them unhurt.

Marigold had regained consciousness once outside and had started in moaning and complaining. She had been taken to the hospital at once though the police were called because of the body. Alain had waited only long enough to be certain that Juliet was alright and then he had gone to be with Marigold.

She was much calmer than she had been two hours before, but Juliet didn't like to think of how long they might have been down in the crypt if Esteban had not been monitoring her through her tracker. Raphael had known she was downstairs, but the elevator had stopped working and everyone else had fled the castle without checking on either him or Bertram, who had been stuck in his room when the quake twisted the stone of his doorway just enough to wedge the wood panel in place. They had also needed rescuing.

Guessing her thoughts, Raphael reached for her hand and squeezed it gently.

"So Smith knew Marigold from before?" Bertram asked, finally unable to contain his curiosity and wanting the full story. "Why did she not recognize him? Was he disguised?"

"Yes, he knew her. But she didn't recognize him because he hid the one feature that would have given him away. It was his eyes. I don't know why he chose to wear contacts. He must have done so all of his life because no one seemed to notice his eyes changing color," Juliet answered after she had swallowed her mouthful of pancakes. Everyone else had ordered dinner, but all she wanted was pancakes with lots of butter and syrup. "Though he may not have known that she was his half-sister. I hope he didn't know. That would make what he did especially beastly."

"He must have known," Esteban said. "Because of the eyes. Why else hide them?"

"Because they were demon green?" Juliet suggested.

119

"They were brother and sister?" Bertram's eyes widened at her revelation.

Raphael did not look shocked at her words, but he had always been rather good at puzzles and could imagine the whole picture from even the few deconstructed pieces she had given him when they were first rescued.

Esteban nodded. He had been more clued in to the investigation than Raphael.

Juliet realized that eventually she would have to explain it all to Scanlon too, but it could wait until morning or even later in the day. The answers had been hidden for five decades, another night wouldn't matter. And Marigold might prefer to tell the story her own way. She should be given the chance.

"It was a pity that she didn't confide in anyone about her real reasons for being at Paul House, though I suppose that it would take a certain amount of nerve to go to the employer you developed a crush on and admit that your mother had been a Satanist, that she had disappeared while living in a squat that happened to be the new jewel in said employer's crown—especially when Mom's body finally turned up down in the crypt and threatened to upset plans for the charity event of the year. And that she had gotten herself hired under false pretenses because she had wanted to play Nancy Drew."

"I suppose. It is the wages of sin." Bertram clearly did not feel that lying to an employer was the kosher thing to do.

Raphael poured him another glass of wine. She thought that Esteban was amused by this naiveté.

"Marigold was lucky that her mother had enough sense to leave her with her sister down in San Jose while she got on with her new life worshipping the infernal master here in the city or she might have died then too," Juliet went on. "Whether Smith's father knew that his girlfriend had given birth to their child, I don't know. I suspect that once he had done his version of Paul on the road to Damascus he may have left San Francisco for a while before going back and trying to convince Marigold's mother that she had to repent her evil ways if she wanted to be saved from the damnation he saw coming. And then 'saving' her in his own special way when she refused to give up her wickedness, perhaps even threatening him with curses or some such nonsense if he tried to block her final initiation into evil."

"Ah. And Smith? Was he there when this evil was happening?"

"Smith was older than Marigold but not by a lot. I assume he was a legitimate child, though he may not have been. In any event, his father infected him early with the same religious paranoia and subsequent perversions of faith. It is possible that he even told Smith bedtime stories about the time he played the role of right hand of God and rid the world of a vile witch while passing the torch of their crusader to the next generation. Since Smith and his father are both dead we will probably never know for sure."

"And Mrs. Smith?"

"Dead, I hope. If not, living somewhere far away from her insane son and ex-husband or lover. Or maybe she was a whack-nut too. That will be for Detective Scanlon to discover."

Juliet sipped her orange juice. She had drunk a lot of water since being rescued but still felt like she needed to wash the dust out of her mouth and throat.

"How did Smith recognize Marigold as his—as the daughter of the Satanist his father killed?"

"Her hair and her necklace. Her eyes too. Also the scent she wore. It was one her mother favored." Juliet sipped her own wine. "I don't know if Marigold honestly thought that she could flush out a killer so many years on. If so, she was completely unprepared to deal with the consequences of finding him. I don't even know if she truly believed that she would discover what had happened to her mother— whose name was Rose Dean, by the way. I think this was a sort of fishing expedition, an effort to close the door on her past. But since she had more or less given up on the idea that she would discover anything definite by the time we arrived, our finding Rose's body shocked her very badly. More than it should have if she truly believed that her mother was dead and hadn't just abandoned her. Mentally, she shut down. She didn't know whom to trust with her secret and she didn't want De Smet to know that this disruption to his plans was caused by her disgraced mother."

"And Mr. Smith?"

"He obviously felt he needed to carry on for dear old dad and keep an eye on Paul House, hence his job at the historical society and his reluctance to allow the renovations. And he decided to act more definitively once Marigold started giving signs of being just like her mother. I think he was trying to make her death look like suicide."

"But you stopped him," Bertram said with satisfaction.

"No, that was an angel and the earthquake," Juliet said, thinking of Smith's crushed head. "I didn't have to do anything. That was delayed retribution."

"Nemesis," Esteban said.

"Yeah. Sometimes karma is a real bitch."

Chapter Ten

Juliet was wearing a favorite medieval gown of stretch velvet and her chain cap which managed to make the outfit seem more roaring twenties than Joan of Arc on her way to be burned, which was how she was feeling in spite of the top-flight canapés and champagne and the rather decent orchestra made up of the most gifted children in the music programs of several local schools.

"Just another hour," she told herself through clenched teeth. Her shoulder still ached a little from the night of the earthquake. The body did not forgive as it once had.

Raphael and Bertram had managed to finish their various repairs and restorations to Paul House in time for the Valentine's Ball, and Juliet had gritted her teeth and stuck it out with them, though she had been bored enough to go off and be a tourist on many of the days when she couldn't pester Raphael into letting her help by cleaning pallets or doing other chores.

Scanlon had been impressed and relieved on the morning after when she gave him the complete story of Addison and Marigold and the sinful fathers and mothers. Between the testimonies offered by Marigold and Juliet, the district attorney, who was also in attendance that night along with the mayor and entire city council, was confident of a conviction if the matter went to trial. Addison Smith was undergoing extensive psychiatric evaluation to determine if he was sane. Juliet didn't think that he was, which was a pity because he needed to be

124

locked up somewhere very unpleasant but also secure.

All that was left for Juliet to do was to smile charmingly at everyone and avoid the press, at least those members who were more interested in psychopaths and earthquake survivors than art. Fortunately, De Smet had managed to screen most of them out before they made it inside. It amused Juliet to see Marigold at his side, playing first lady. She thought that it was partially guilt that made De Smet seek her company so often these days, but there was no denying that being looked at with blind adoration could also be part of why he had asked her to be hostess that evening.

"Miss Henry," said Detective Scanlon, who had found a tux and was wearing it rather well though Juliet thought the gardenia in the buttonhole made the outfit border on burlesque.

Of course, that might have been his intention. She doubted that he was there by choice.

"Detective. How goes the war?" Juliet smiled her first genuine smile of the night.

"As ever. I shall never run out of work in this town."

"But nothing too exotic or ancient on the desk these days?"

"No, it has all been blessedly routine and present day. By the way, if I forgot to say thank you before, then let me do it now. I don't think this case would have been broken without you and the chef would very likely be dead had you not intervened. I hope she has expressed her gratitude." He sounded skeptical.

Marigold had thanked her too. When they were rescued and she was being loaded into the ambulance. She had since forgotten that it was Juliet and Esteban and the fire department, not Alain De Smet, who had seen to her liberation from durance vile.

"You did thank me," Juliet said. "Your mother must have raised you right. She should be proud."

"I'll pass the compliment on when I see her next." Scanlon took a sip of his champagne. He didn't seem that impressed and Juliet was sure that he was more of a beer drinker. "Who is the man with your Raphael James? He looks terribly important."

"The one who looks like a foreign potentate? He is. He thinks. Don't look now, but he is some kind of royalty, or at least someone titled. The *gentilhomme* has just inherited a chateau and is trying to convince Raphael that he should come and make it look all seventeenth-century, pre-guillotine elegant again."

"Will he succeed?" Scanlon asked. "Your Mr. James has a very good poker face. I can't guess what he is thinking."

Scanlon was right. Raphael also looked rather regal, a king on his throne.

"If the project is interesting enough and the price is right he may get what he wants. Raphael does not enjoy traveling as much these days. It offends his dignity to be subjected to special security screenings because of his chair. It will have to be something spectacular to tempt him."

126

Unfortunately, Juliet was sure the chateau was spectacular. Or could be if Raphael took on the project.

"I don't think anyone does like travel these days. But at what price freedom? People want to be safe."

"Safe from what?" Juliet asked tartly and then forced herself to smile again. "Sorry, Detective Scanlon. I am a bit tired."

"Miss Henry, one might think that you weren't enjoying yourself here with the rich and famous."

Scanlon looked amused.

"I'm not, but will pretend to be happy if it kills me."

"Why? Because of Mr. James? Or the press?" he guessed.

"Yes, but mostly because of that man over by the ridiculously large fan of gladioli. The one with the small glasses and mean eyes."

"The tall, red flowers by the door?" Scanlon asked, looking toward the entrance. "He does look a bit … out of place. Is he a bodyguard?"

"No. That is a colleague of the not-so-charming gentleman who visited your office a few weeks ago. Only he is much less charming than Peter Davis. He or his clones turn up periodically at art shows and other events to stare at me."

"Why? Are they harassing you?"

"I'm sure they don't see it that way. It is more in the way of checking up to see if I am ready to go back to the salt mine and work for the devil."

"Ah. And you still aren't ready?" he asked.

"I am not."

"Well, smile harder. Here comes Mr. James and he looks very chipper. At a guess, you'll be going to France soon."

Juliet did smile at Raphael, but it wasn't hard.

"Having fun?" she asked as Scanlon faded away in the general direction away from the gladioli.

"After a fashion. And you, Juliet? You have survived the night? I have not seen much of you."

"I am also enjoying it after a fashion. You should be proud of your work." Her eyes went to the man by the gladioli and Raphael followed her gaze. "Perhaps I am enjoying it slightly less than you though."

"Ah. Has he approached you?"

"Not yet."

"Could I interest you in a long vacation in France?"

"The French chateau?" she asked and then shook her head, feeling a little sad that she wouldn't see Raphael for a long while but very determined not to be persuaded. "No thanks. With my luck, it will be chock-o-block with corpses, missing jewels, and terrorists. I am going home to my cat where I can eat tuna fish sandwiches and not find a dead body every week."

"I thought you might feel that way," Raphael said. "That is in part why I declined the project."

Juliet was surprised.

"Really? You said no? I should have thought that this would be right up your alley."

Raphael spread his hands.

"It is, but Monsieur Saint-Simon is rather tedious and interfering since he thinks he knows about art. But I also want to go home to the cat and tuna fish sandwiches, and not find a body every week. We have rather had a surfeit of corpses these last two months. I need a rest."

"Then you're on," Juliet said, feeling genuinely happy for the first time in a month. "We can even leave tonight if you want. I wouldn't mind the drive and I am mostly packed anyway."

"Very well. Let us say our farewells to Mr. De Smet and depart. We have done our bit for the cause and Monsieur Saint-Simon grows more importunate by the hour."

"Raphael, I thought you'd never ask. I'll even help you pack."

"It is already done. I knew you would not want to stay."

About the Author

Melanie Jackson is the author of over 100 novels and novellas. If you enjoyed this book, please visit Melanie's author web site at www.melaniejackson.com. She has a newsletter where she makes special offers for series readers. She also loves to hear from readers and can be contacted at mjjaxn@gmail.com

eBooks by Melanie Jackson:

The Chloe Boston Mystery Series:
Moving Violation
The Pumpkin Thief
Death in a Turkey Town
Murder on Parade
Cupid's Revenge
Viva Lost Vegas
Death of a Dumb Bunny
Red, White and a Dog Named Blue
Haunted
The Great Pumpkin Caper
Beast of a Feast
Snow Angel
Lucky Thirteen
The Sham
Murder by the Book
Cornucopia
Make Over
On the Beach
Camp Chaos
The Davenport Caper

Up in the Air
Cooked Books

The Butterscotch Jones Mystery Series
Due North
Big Bones
Gone South
Home Fires
Points West
The Wedding
Wild East
Still Waters

The Wendover House Mystery Series
The Secret Staircase
Twelfth Night
On Deadly Tides
Pieces of Hate
Mysterious Island

Miss Henry Mystery Series
Portrait of a Gossip
Landscape in Scarlet
Requiem at Christmas
Impression of Bones
Blue Period
Memento Mori
Eye of the Beholder
Drowning Pool
Modern Art

Kenneth Mayhew Series
Mayhem Mansion

On the Rocks
Overboard

Historical Mystery
Death in a High Place
Death in a Low Place

Wildside Series
Traveler
Outsiders
Courier
Still Life
The Master
The Saint

The Divine Series
Divine Fire
Divine Madness
Divine Night
Divine Fantasy
Nevermore

The Book of Dreams Series:
The First Book of Dreams: Metropolis
The Second Book of Dreams: Meridian
The Third Book of Dreams: Destiny

Medicine Trilogy
Bad Medicine
Medicine Man
Knave of Hearts

Paranormal Romance

Night Visitor
Dominion
The Selkie
The Selkie Bride
Writ on Water
And They Danced
A Curious Affair
The Curiosity Shoppe (Sequel to a Curious Affair)
The Night Side
The Ghost and Miss Demure
Club Valhalla
Timeless (Sequel to Club Valhalla)

Scottish Historical Romance
Devil of Bodmin Moor
Devil of the Highlands
Devil in a Red Coat

Halloween
A Cozy Christmas

40448507R00078

Made in the USA
Lexington, KY
08 April 2015